Whose Dog Are You?

The Reward Game
The Revenge Game
Fair Game
The Game
Cousin Once Removed
Sauce for the Pigeon
Pursuit of Arms
Silver City Scandal
The Executor
The Worried Widow
Adverse Report
Stray Shot
Dog in the Dark
A Brace of Skeet

Whose Dog Are You?

Gerald Hammond

//

St. Martin's Press
New York

Library of Congress Cataloging-in-Publication Data

Hammond, Gerald.
    Whose dog are you? / Gerald Hammond.
      p.   cm.
    ISBN 0-312-05536-6
    I. Title.
    PR6058.A55456W48   1991
    823'.914—dc20   90-15534
                                           CIP

First published in Great Britain by Macmillan London Limited.

First U.S. Edition: April 1991
10 9 8 7 6 5 4 3 2 1

I am his Highness' dog at Kew;
Pray tell me, sir, whose dog are you?

*On the Collar of a Dog which I gave to his Royal
Highness.*
Alexander Pope.

One

There are no prizes for guessing almost right. With a gale blasting out of the south-west I expected the geese to come low off the reserve and struggle upstream, to leave the river somewhere around the old treestumps beyond the first bend; but in the colourless light of dawn they had come in a single skein, calling to each other as they fought the wind and passing well to our left and more than a gunshot high on their way to the feeding grounds.

Beth stirred beside me in the mud below the river bank. 'Is that it?' she asked hopefully.

'Probably,' I said. 'But we'll hang on a little longer.'

Beth subsided with an audible squelch and an equally audible sigh. She had insisted on coming with me as firmly as I had insisted on the expedition. I had missed most of the wildfowling season due to a recurrence of the illness which had ended my army career and nearly killed me. A very mild recurrence – the parasite had been identified and dealt with although the organic damage remained – but one conveniently (from Beth's viewpoint) serious enough to restrict the outings which had always worried her, without much hampering my work in our joint business.

Now that I was back as near to perfect health as I dared hope for, I was determined to shake off the bonds of invalidism. One of my great pleasures had always been the foreshore at dawn, watching the water coming to life and waiting in the growing light in the hope that today, for once, I had got it right and that the geese would come over me within shot. The pursuit was all, the occasional shot was immaterial. Now, with the season about to close, it was go or wait seven months.

Honouring an old agreement, Beth made only slight objection. But knowing how vulnerable to the cold was my underweight frame and also fearing a return of my occasional blackouts, she determined to accompany me. To her surprise, I agreed. Not only did she have a point; I was confident that she would be oblivious to the magic of wildfowling and only too conscious of the discomforts, and would leave me to pursue that activity in cheerful solitude thereafter.

Daylight was almost complete. There were colours to be seen now, the muted colours of winter on the east coast of Scotland. It seemed that the last of the geese had passed. Any late-comers could be trusted to give vocal warning of their approach. I turned to face any duck which might be heading to roost after feeding overnight. Already the bottle-shapes of a few mallard had passed over, high and fast, and I had only recognised a merganser just in time to stop myself shooting a protected species. A merganser, seen head or tail on, can look very like a mallard.

'The tide's coming closer,' Beth said.

'You've got my waders on,' I pointed out. 'You won't dissolve.' It was against the hunter's instinct to go home with clean barrels. But then I relented. 'When it reaches us, we'll go,' I said.

A spring of a dozen or more teal came at me suddenly, downwind, fast and low. Rather than risk my heavy goose load reducing a bird to shreds of flesh and bloodstained feathers I turned round again and was just in time to drop a tail-ender in mid-river.

'You can send Jason,' I said. Jason is Beth's personal

Labrador and the only one of our many dogs privileged to risk his life in tidal waters. The others, all springer spaniels, were the breeding stock of a working kennels.

Beth gave the word and Jason went out, throwing up a bow-wave like that of a destroyer. I heard the deep grunt as he gathered his quarry. The little duck seemed lost in his big mouth. He surged back and presented Beth with a cock teal.

She thanked him politely, without enthusiasm. She loves to work Jason but she was obviously disappointed. 'Is this all?' she said. 'It's only a baby!'

'It's fully grown,' I said. 'It's a small species but very tasty.'

'Not much of a return for getting out of bed before the crack of dawn, driving umpteen miles, staggering more miles through a howling gale in the dark and then squishing around in the freezing mud.'

'Good for the complexion,' I said. 'Keep telling yourself that it's fun, fun, fun.'

Stung by the suggestion that her complexion could benefit from a mud pack, Beth would probably have made a hot retort. Instead, she uttered a scream which put up a pair of shelduck from under the far bank. I thought at first that she was giving vent to indignation until I saw in the strengthening light that her eyes were round and scared. I looked where she seemed to be looking.

Ten yards upstream of us, the body of a man was grounded face-down at the edge of the mud. Not much more showed than a hump of shoulder and the line of a leg but there was on doubting what it was. Below the water, lank hair of indeterminate colour floated as if raised in fear and the wavelets caused his hips to rise and fall in an obscene parody of the sexual act.

'You'd better go to the phone,' I said.

'But— '

'You wouldn't rather stay here and watch him while I go?'

White-faced, Beth shook her head. 'Couldn't we both go?'

'He might drift away again. The tide brought him up but the wind could take him down.'

I helped her to extricate herself from the mud and gave her the key of the car. 'Go back to the bridge,' I said. 'I think there's a phone-box somewhere. If not, knock on somebody's door. Call the police and tell them that there's a body. You can leave Jason with me,' I added.

'All right,' Beth whispered.

'You can manage?'

'I'll have to,' she said bravely. She gave a little shiver and then surprised me by asking whether I was warm enough. Before we left the house, Beth had stood over me while I donned everything from thermal underwear to thick sweaters, so I was able to answer honestly that I was, if anything, too hot.

'Well, stay warm,' she said, 'and don't do anything silly.'

She took one more horrified glance at the object at the water's edge and set off, the hood of her anorak flapping like a demented bird in the wind.

As she neared the bridge I would again be in her view. While she was out of sight I took the opportunity to examine the body. It had been in the water for some time. The River Eden and its estuary have bottoms mainly of mud and sand but there is enough stony ground to do a lot of damage to a body which is being carried up and down by the tide.

I had had enough to do with bodies during my army service to know not to move it by a limb. If the body had been a body for long enough, the limb could come away in your hand. Perhaps I was becoming soft in civilian life. Most of the clothes had suffered as much as

10

the flesh. He had lost his boots and trouser-legs and yet, incongruously, a silver dog-whistle on a chain still hung around his neck. His waxed cotton coat was unzipped but had stood up to immersion and abrasion remarkably well. I took hold of the collar to move him.

When I was sure that the body was far enough on to the mud not to drift away again, I settled back under the bank. I thought that I would probably have an hour before the police arrived and there might still be another teal to add to the bag.

The police, as is their custom, showed far more consideration for the dead than for the living. They had taken an unconscionable time over arriving, taking possession of the body and obtaining a preliminary statement from me. And then, when I returned to the car in the pub car park, Beth had already warmed the engine in order to heat a towel — not for my benefit but in order to dry Jason.

It was mid-morning before we arrived home. Home is Three Oaks, a converted farmhouse set in the hilly farmland of northern Fife and a few acres of garden whose landscaping would look better for the absence of blocks of kennels, each with its outdoor run, and many, many dogs to tear up the grass and dig beneath the shrubs. Despite these handicaps Beth, with occasional help from me, usually managed to keep the place neat and even colourful.

Isobel, the third member of our partnership, was understandably fretful. (At any time during the previous few months she would have been furious at being left to manage the chores on her own, but with the ending of the field trials season we had entered one of the few comparatively leisurely periods of our year.) Isobel Kitts, plump and bespectacled and given to wearing woolly cardigans, could have been mistaken for any unobtrusive

11

lady of late middle age but, when you looked into the depths of her character, highlights and shadows began to show. She had her faults, among them the habit of marking any high or low spot in her life by going on an alcoholic spree, but against that, as a qualified vet who always kept our stock in prime condition, a tireless worker and a natural-born handler of dogs under competition conditions, she was worth her weight in Supreme Dual Champions.

Beth broke in on Isobel's mild reproaches. 'Yes,' she said. 'But we found a *body*. A dead one. You couldn't expect us to come rushing back here. I had to squelch back to Guardbridge and phone the police.'

'You could have phoned me at the same time,' Isobel pointed out.

'John didn't give me any money.'

Isobel helped herself to coffee. We were in the big kitchen of Three Oaks by then and Beth was conversing over her shoulder while whipping up a late but welcome breakfast. The dead body, it seemed, was of more interest than our thoughtless behaviour, because Isobel forebore from demolishing Beth's excuses. 'Whose body was it?' she asked, pushing back the ungainly spectacles on her nose. 'Anybody I'd know?'

'I shouldn't think so,' I said. I had taken off my heavy coat and leggings, but the warmth of the kitchen was reminding me that I was still overdressed. I stripped off a sweater while I wondered how to phrase it. 'He hadn't been in the water for less than a week,' I said at last. 'And he'd taken quite a beating, being rolled around on the bottom. It could have been anybody.'

'But male?'

'From what I could see,' I said. 'It wasn't my business to examine him. I expect the police will identify him from the list of permit-holders.'

Beth put a plate of eggs, bacon, sausages, tomatoes

12

and mushrooms in front of me, with a piece of fried bread to keep it company and toast on the side. A rush of saliva prevented any further disclosures for the moment. Beth only tolerated my wildfowling trips because of their effect on my usually wayward appetite.

'What makes you so sure that he was a wildfowler?' Isobel asked. 'He could have been an airman who walked over the edge of the Leuchars Airbase in the dark, or a golfer who couldn't bear to live with his handicap another moment.'

Beth sat down more decorously with her own meal. 'I only saw him for a few seconds,' she said, 'but I did see that he was wearing a cartridge belt.'

'Ah!' Isobel nodded and looked wise. 'That would weigh him down. I expect that's why he hadn't been found sooner. All the same, he could have been brought down from further up the river.'

I had satisfied the first agonies of hunger. I emptied my mouth. 'It gets pretty shallow before Dairsie,' I said. 'And the river was low today. Of course, it may have been higher when he fell in.'

I cleaned my plate in silence and began on the toast.

'What sort of cartridges did he have in the belt?' Beth asked suddenly.

'They weren't magnums,' I said, 'if that's what you mean. But yes, I did take a look at one of them. Loaded with number three shot.'

'Wildfowler!' Beth said triumphantly. 'Probably cut off by the tide. You read about them.'

I took off my second sweater and tossed it in the general direction of one of the fireside chairs. 'I don't think you've ever read about them on the Eden,' I said. 'It happens on the Wash or the Solway, places where you can go squishing out for miles over the mud and the gutters can fill behind you if you don't have one eye on your watch and the other on the tide tables.

13

Where we were, the river isn't very wide. And most of the estuary's flat.'

'He could have got lost and walked in a circle,' Isobel said.

'He couldn't get disoriented. He'd only have to keep heading away from the water. Anyway,' I said, 'you couldn't get lost on the Eden mudflats even in a sudden fog. If you couldn't see the lights of St Andrews, you'd have the noise of the traffic on the main road, the Tannoy at the paperworks at Guardbridge and a whole NATO airbase along the north shore. It's the noisiest wildfowling ground I ever came across. I don't know how the birds put up with it.'

'Will we have to give evidence at an enquiry?' Beth asked.

'Unless he turns out to be a clear case of a heart attack there'll probably be a fatal accident enquiry,' I said. Inquests are not held in Scotland. 'One of us will have to give evidence about finding the body. You can do it. You saw him first.'

Beth gave a little shiver. 'I couldn't,' she said quickly. 'You saw him only two seconds later. And you saw more of him. It's odd that we haven't heard anything about a missing wildfowler.'

'It may have been some ass who came from miles away without telling anybody where he was going,' I said. 'They've probably been looking for him in all the wrong places. I suppose it's even possible that the body was swept round from Tentsmuir.'

Beth shivered again. 'I don't think I want to talk about it any more,' she said. 'If you've finished, we've got pups to feed and young dogs to train.'

'And I've got accounts to get out,' Isobel added. 'So clear the table before you go.' The so-called office was totally cluttered with Isobel's records so that our accounts were usually dealt with on the kitchen table.

The wind had eased or else we were more sheltered now that we were away from the coast. The day had turned mild for mid-February. I got rid of the thermal vest before starting work. And then it was back to the old routine. Feed and clean and teach. Wash the feeding dishes and start again. But the monotony was tolerable, even comforting.

I had had my moment of escape, pitting my wits and skill against the creatures of the wild. The fact that only one small teal had failed to outwit me did nothing to diminish the thrill of the hunt. And whatever sensation may be experienced after the finding of a dead body, it is never one of boredom.

Late the following day, a Friday, a uniformed sergeant from Cupar arrived at Three Oaks. I had met him before over the renewal of my shotgun certificate and Sergeant Ewell had struck me as both patient and also more knowledgeable about dogs and shooting than many of his kind. He had a thin face which looked ready to smile although I had never seen it do so and I thought that the grey in his hair was premature, probably from dealing with idiots like me. His uniform always looked spruce enough for duty outside a royal palace. His voice was soft although I thought that he could be a hard man with villains. I liked him without quite knowing why. Somewhere within our dealings lay the indefinable seed of friendship.

The Sergeant had brought a statement, embodying all that I had told his colleagues the previous day, for my signature; but when I had signed it he was in no hurry to depart. He settled in one of the pair of soft chairs which occupy a corner of the big kitchen, accepted a mug of tea and prepared for a chat. Jason, who had taken an unaccustomed fancy to him, planted a broad head on the Sergeant's knee. The Sergeant, who seemed to be

15

at home with dogs, scratched him behind the ear in just the way that reduced Jason to a state of adoring imbecility.

I had noticed during our earlier encounters that the Sergeant always seemed ready for conversation. I had wondered whether this was his nature or a conscious ploy; and how much useful information he gathered over the innocent teacups. This time, however, I could see that he was thinking harder than our idle chatter warranted and I guessed that he was waiting for his chance to introduce some chosen topic. So when we had said what there was to say about the weather, the prospects for the local farmers and the traffic on the main road, I asked him, 'Have they found out who the man is yet?'

He brightened. 'Not to my knowledge,' he said. 'My brother-in-law's in Kirkcaldy and he's senior to me. He's kept me posted. The last he told me, they were hoping that his fingerprints might be on record, or that the pathologist would come up with something useful – scars or diseases or unusual stomach contents.'

'His fingertips were badly messed up,' I said.

'Aye. But the fingerprint patterns are repeated on the underskin, what they call the dermis. They got a few wee bits of prints, I'm told.'

Beth was away, fetching fresh supplies of kennel meal and dried meat and at the same time acclimatising some of the younger dogs to travel by car. But Isobel, who had taken the older dogs on a training walk, came in with some papers while the Sergeant was speaking and settled at the kitchen table. The Sergeant fell silent but Isobel laughed at him. 'You can go on talking,' she said. 'I'm not squeamish. And I'm not a gossip.'

'Both quite true,' I said. 'Didn't they get anything from the man's pockets?'

'His trouser pockets had ripped although they were

16

jeans. He didn't have a jacket, just a thick sweater. There was a small compass in the pocket of his coat, a handkerchief, thirty pence in silver and one fired cartridge.'

'And a whistle round his neck,' I said. 'Has the warden come across a shot bird?'

'No. But that means nothing. He could have missed,' the Sergeant pointed out. 'Or a bird could have been carried out to sea. Or another fowler could have picked it up.'

'The thirty pence suggests that he'd come across the Tay Bridge,' Isobel said, 'and he had the coins ready for going back.'

'Not necessarily.' My Barbour coat was hanging on the back of my chair. I reached round and felt in the right-hand pocket, producing forty-five pence. 'I keep enough for the bridge toll and the car park machine in my coat pocket, ready for the next time.'

'You were a Boy Scout,' Isobel said. 'You'll arrive in Heaven with a condom in your pocket, just in case.' (Sergeant Ewell's eyes opened wide. He had not encountered Isobel's bluntness before.) 'He still sounds like a wildfowler to me. But his gun hasn't been found?'

'It would soon cover with mud,' I said. 'He could have winged a bird and, not having a dog, tried to recover it himself. Or if his dog seemed to be in difficulties he might have gone to the rescue. A dog often looks as if it's on the point of drowning although they almost never do. But that's one way he could have drowned.'

'M'hm,' said the Sergeant. He paused. 'There's one other thing. Just one . . .'

'Out with it,' Isobel said briskly. 'You don't have to be coy. Was he wearing lace panties under the jeans?'

'Nothing like that,' the Sergeant said hastily. He seemed deeply shocked. 'It may have nothing to do with

17

the mannie in the water, mind, but then again it may. Mr Cunningham mentioned a dog or the lack of one, and the man did have a whistle on him. There's a spaniel bitch was brought in this morning. Apparently she's been hanging around the houses on the golf course the last week or two, scrounging for food and stealing from dustbins, but they didn't think of fetching her in to the police station until today. No collar,' the Sergeant added severely.

'Well, she wouldn't have a collar,' Isobel said. She had half turned in her chair, her papers quite forgotten. 'Not if he − or somebody − was shooting. Collars get caught up in things. Dogs can be drowned or strangled that way.'

The Sergeant was nodding. 'I was wondering ... You're spaniel folk. Would there be any way you could tell where she came from?'

I kept my mouth shut. Isobel could almost be seen to prick up her ears. She is our expert on gundog breeding and congenital faults. It is not a field which often has links with forensic science, but she and her husband Henry were devotees of mystery stories and plays. 'There could be,' she said. 'It depends. Where could we get a look at her?'

'I said you'd be willing to help. I have her in the car outside. She's an amiable wee beast.'

'Bring her inside then,' Isobel said.

'Aye.' But the Sergeant sat where he was, fondling Jason's ear. 'There's just one other thing ... ' It seemed to be his favourite expression. 'She's coming into season.'

Isobel made a face. 'In that case, some ghastly hybrid's probably served her already. We'll come out with you.'

The Sergeant got to his feet. 'I don't think so. Her hinder parts are a wee bit puffy but there's no sign of colour yet.'

18

We followed him out to his panda car. A small liver and white springer was curled on the back seat. We looked at her through the car's window. The tip of her stump of a tail twitched.

'Working strain,' I said. A show springer would have been larger, with a longer head and almost certainly more neuroses.

'Obviously,' Isobel said. She had brought a lead out with her. The Sergeant unlocked the car and the bitch accepted the lead and emerged cautiously, sniffing the air. The scent must have been reassuring, carrying traces of many contented dogs. When we made no threatening moves, she relaxed. She sat at Isobel's feet and waited for whatever fate might bring. She was in a poor state, her coat matted and dirty. Her body was thin, which made it easier for Isobel gently to feel her joints. The bitch sat still, comforted rather than disturbed by the touch.

'Well?' said Sergeant Ewell.

'Give us a chance,' Isobel said. She was looking into the spaniel's sad eyes. 'No congenital defects. But even if I knew her, I wouldn't recognise her in this state.'

'Markings mean very little,' I explained, 'unless they're very distinctive. Can you leave her over the weekend at the very least? When she's been cleaned up and if she's settled down a bit, we may be able to tell you something about her.'

The Sergeant made a small sound of relief. 'I was hoping you'd say that.' He paused, showing a trace of embarrassment. 'This is the way of it. I'm doing this off my own bat. If I can produce a lead to the man's identity, that'd be noticed by the highheidyins.'

'And be remembered when the time for promotions came round?' Isobel said, smiling. 'We understand.'

'That's just how it is.' He looked down at his shining toecaps. 'At that time, the bosses are more likely to remember the men at HQ whose work and faces have been in front of them. Out here in the wilds, you have to struggle to be noticed. Ever since her brother went up to inspector my wife's been on at me, asking why I'm still only a sergeant and when I'm going to be made up.' He sighed and then straightened his back, recovering the dignity which he had let slip. 'I'll let St Andrews know. If anyone turns up to claim her, they'll send them to you.'

'With a written authorisation I trust,' Isobel said. 'She may belong to someone in St Andrews. On the other hand, you have the unidentified body of a shooting man and a gundog which seems to have been on the loose for a week or two. Some connection is at least possible. If she belonged to the dead man, there may be argument over his estate. I'm not handing over a possibly valuable bitch to the first person who knocks on the door. If I did that, she'd surely turn out to be a champion of champions and worth the mint. Sod's Law,' she added.

The Sergeant very nearly smiled. 'You'll get your written authorisation,' he said. 'Don't let her go without it.'

'We won't.'

He gave the spaniel a farewell pat and got into his car. As he moved off, Isobel asked me, 'What sort of whistle was the corpse wearing? Silent?'

'No. Take one of those ordinary whistles out of the shop, the silver ones by Richards of Birmingham. If it wasn't the same it was damn near it.'

The panda car was hardly out of sight before my big and rust-streaked estate car turned into the drive. I went out to help Beth unload.

'I crossed with Sergeant Ewell in the village,' she said. 'Had he been here? What was it? A summons to appear at a fatal accident enquiry?'

'According to the paper, the enquiry's been put off to allow more time for enquiries,' I told her. I began to explain but Beth, for once, was not inclined to delve into a mystery. As soon as I mentioned the new arrival it was the state of the bitch which concerned her and she bore the little springer away for an immediate bath, a good feed and the removal of several ticks which had flourished in the unkempt coat, leaving me to transfer three young spaniels back to their kennels and carry bags of foodstuffs into the house.

The results of Beth's labour were to be seen by late afternoon.

Isobel and I had undertaken the main feed in order to leave Beth free, but we had knocked off at dusk for a drink and a planning meeting in the sitting room. Two of our brood bitches were due in season within the next couple of months but one of these was a daughter of Samson, our resident stud, and we had decided, after lengthy debate, against inbreeding. The coffee table was piled with extracts from Isobel's records of past performances while we debated the choice of an alternative husband of suitable pedigree. We had settled on the best contender, subject to the agreement of a suitable dowry, and had moved on to the question of gundog working tests in the coming months. These do not carry the status of field trials but they can be useful qualifiers.

Henry, Isobel's husband, joined us, having walked the mile or two from their home. Henry was some years older than Isobel – who, when narked, was wont to say that he was well past his sell-by date – but I would hope to be half as spry and vigorous if I ever manage to reach his age. Henry's share in our venture had been limited to providing Isobel's share of the capital, but he was a good friend, a fount of sound advice and an invaluable standby whenever we found ourselves short-handed.

Beth and the unnamed springer found us indulging in chat and a modest drink. Beth was not usually slow to demand a small sherry when any kind of festivity is in progress, but on this occasion she waved it away. 'How does this grab you?' she demanded.

The question was clearly rhetorical. The springer bitch showed no inclination to grab anybody, she was far too busy showing herself off to the company. She had been shampooed and blow-dried and then brushed until she shone. A smell of Antimate followed her into the room. She was still thin, but most gundogs are lean at the end of the season. A breadth around her lower ribs suggested that a substantial meal had been gratefully received.

She was on her third circuit of the company, demanding and receiving our approval and petting, when Isobel suddenly said 'Hup!'

The bitch sat.

'So she's trained to traditional spaniel commands,' I said. I usually have a few rubber balls around for indoor training in miniature and when I rolled one of these into a corner she followed it with her eyes and sat tight. But when I said 'Get on,' she looked at me in puzzlement.

'Hie lost,' said Isobel. No reaction.

Henry said 'Fetch,' and the spaniel darted into the corner and brought him the ball. 'Languages are a gift,' Henry said complacently as he accepted it.

Beth had relaxed now that her protégée had been duly admired. She asked for a sherry and settled beside Henry on the settee. I topped up all our glasses. The fire had burned up and the room, which could look cheerless at times, danced to the tune of the flames.

'That doesn't tell us much,' Isobel said, 'except that she's been trained as if for the gun.'

'Or for obedience tests,' I said.

'Yes, and words of command are too damned idiosyncratic. But at least we can give her a workout.' Isobel stared through her spectacles until the springer showed signs of bashfulness and retired behind my legs. 'I keep thinking I've seen her before. Competing, I'm sure. But markings are a snare and a delusion; she'll need some time to get her figure back and Beth's got her tarted up like a show freak. If I could see her working . . . '

'We could go out to the barn,' I suggested.

Isobel shook her greying head firmly. 'Let her settle down over the weekend. Put her in the isolation kennel with another quiet bitch and we'll give her a test on Monday. I want to see how she works thick cover. Henry can come and be the other Gun, can't you, Henry? May as well get as close to field trial conditions as is possible out of season.'

'Delighted,' Henry said. He paused and looked at me pop-eyed. 'Could that body have been in the water for as long as a month?' he asked. Isobel would certainly have given him the few details which we knew and Henry was visibly pleased to get his teeth into a mystery which was not fictitious.

'You'd have to ask the pathologist,' I said. 'But I'd have thought not. Why?'

'Because I looked in my diary. That's how long it is since we've had heavy rain. We don't have a lot of mountains to hold the water, this side of the Tay. The spate arrives quickly and drops as quickly.'

'We made up our minds that the man was a wildfowler,' Beth said. 'Who else would be using such large shot?'

'Somebody who was out at night, lamping a fox.'

'You do talk a lot of nonsense sometimes,' Isobel said indulgently. 'Anyone after a fox at night would be local, so the police would know if he'd gone missing. And he had a compass in his pocket. Only wildfowlers carry compasses.'

'But no permit to shoot on the Eden,' Henry said.

'It was probably in a trouser pocket,' I said. 'They were ripped.'

Henry nodded slowly and took a pull at his beer. 'So he was a wildfowler,' he said at last. 'So where's his car?'

'In St Andrews, gathering parking tickets,' Beth said. 'They'll find it. Come along, you,' she added to the spaniel. 'Out to the isolation kennel before you get too used to being a house-dog like that lazy lump of mine.'

Two

Henry and Isobel walked from their home on the Monday morning, Henry with his old gun slung in a sleeve over his shoulder. Each looked mildly hung over. They were a sociable pair but inclined to go over the top and for them Sunday night was usually party night.

Demarcation disputes were unknown in the partnership, but although we tried to remain flexible – we took rather a pride in our interchangeability – we tended to have our own specialities. I was the trainer. Isobel, who had the knack of thinking calmly in the stress of competition, did most of the handling in field trials; as a former vet, she oversaw the health of our stock; and much of the paperwork fell to her.

Beth had come to us as kennelmaid and had progressed rapidly to being mistress, partner, fiancée and, quite recently, my wife. She could and sometimes did train and handle the dogs as competently as any of us, but she stayed responsible for all the wearying tasks of the kennelmaid. She had taken a pride in restoring the newcomer to a good condition and she would have liked to see her in action. Her eyes followed us as we left for The Moss. The pups had been fed but the runs still had to be cleaned and the dogs exercised; and we tried never to leave the place unguarded or the phone unmanned.

We walked the half mile to The Moss. The day was dry and bright but cold. In view of her season the little spaniel was reeking of Antimate and almost rattling with Amplex tablets and we kept her on a lead until we reached The Moss. She stayed faithfully at heel but gave an occasional little dance of impatience. More than ever I was convinced that she had been trained to the gun. It was our habit to introduce the dogs' mealtimes by firing a shot with the dummy launcher or a blank cartridge pistol – a trick which, by associating the sound of a shot in the dogs' minds with their favourite experience, made gunshyness at a later stage unknown. At the sound, she had sat firmly – a basic step in gundog training.

Lacking any other name, we had christened the little spaniel bitch Anon. As we walked the rough ground, Isobel sent her out and she worked a good pattern ahead of us. Words of command posed an occasional problem but hand signals are universal.

Gamebirds, being out of season and aware of it, had mostly returned to their home coverts but a single cock pheasant exploded up, gaudy in the bright sunlight. Henry, on Isobel's other side, fired a shot in the air. Anon sat quickly. The pheasant accelerated and sailed on, no doubt blessing Henry for his poor marksmanship.

So far so good.

It was another of our habits to save a few pheasants, unplucked, in the freezer against just such occasions. Beth had thawed one the day before. I dropped the bird surreptitiously in a clump of bracken and we walked on. From a hundred yards, Isobel handled Anon back. Anon responded at a good pace and soon found the bird. She was expecting a freshly shot bird and jibbed for a moment at the less familiar scent, but lifted it and came trotting back, head held high.

'Does that tell you anything?' I asked Isobel. I put the pheasant back in my game-bag. Dinner tonight would be special.

'Give me time.'

An outbreak of myxomatosis had reduced the rabbit population to nearly zero, but the stunted trees in the middle of The Moss were on a flightline of woodpigeon between their roosting trees on the hilltop and a big rape-field near the village. We tucked ourselves into hiding among the branches of small conifers. Twenty minutes and six cartridges brought four pigeon and four good retrieves.

We set off for home, glad to be on the move. Standing still, we had felt the bite of the cold.

'She's met woodies before,' Henry said.

Isobel grunted. The comment was too obvious to need a reply. Woodpigeon are strongly scented and loose-feathered. Many dogs dislike lifting them at first. 'Pity about the rabbits,' she said. 'I'd have liked to try her on ground game. I'm sure there was something . . .'

'We can see how she behaves in the rabbit pen,' I said.

'It's not the same thing in a pen,' Isobel said.

The removal of a nearby tennis club, when the District Council had provided better facilities in the area, had enabled us to complete our facilities with the rabbit pen. The perimeter wiring had been transferred, by dint of colossal labour, to enclose half an acre of unused garden behind the house where bushes and weeds could be left to riot. The enclosed area had then been stocked with rabbits, both wild and domestic, fortunately before disease struck the local population; and so far our captives had resisted infection. The pen had turned out to be the most useful training facility of all. Chasing fur is an almost irresistible temptation to any dog, but regular training in the rabbit pen enabled us to sell our dogs warranted 'steady to fur'. It was then up to the purchasers to keep them that way. Few of them managed to do so, but that was hardly our fault.

Beth must have been watching for our return. She met us with mugs of hot soup against the cold of the day and we carried them with us to the pen. I detoured by way of the kitchen garden to pull up some greens.

When I caught up with the others, Isobel was already in the pen. Anon was tight against Isobel's leg. From time to time I saw her coat ripple as she gave a small shiver. A large, white rabbit, donated to us when a neighbouring family moved away, watched with pink eyes, quite unafraid.

Beth turned away from the wire. 'She doesn't want to know about rabbits,' she said to me. 'It's as if she's afraid of them. She's more nervous than they are. How odd!'

'You'd better come out,' I said to Isobel.

I tossed my harvest of cauliflower leaves inside for the benefit of the rabbits and we adjourned to the lawn. A few minutes' work with dummies confirmed our first suspicion. The spaniel bitch worked perfectly on canvas dummies but refused to touch any that were covered with rabbit-skin.

'She's been corrected for chasing,' I said, 'and somebody's used too heavy a hand.'

Isobel had been very quiet but suddenly she snapped her fingers. 'Got it!' she said. 'I knew I'd seen the beggar before. Let's go inside.'

Beth went to put Anon back in the isolation kennel. When she caught up with us, Isobel was leafing through back numbers of sporting magazines on the kitchen table and I was making a pot of tea.

Isobel muttered as she flicked over the pages – whether to us or to herself I could not be sure. 'More than a year ago . . . it was a trial at Elmhill, which makes it November or December . . . somebody from Ayrshire way . . . performed beautifully . . . then she was put out for failing on a rabbit and let me through into second place with Starlight . . . otherwise she'd have . . . ' Isobel stopped and slapped the page. 'Here it is. She even

28

appears in a group photograph. Salmon of Glevedale. Rotten name, but no wonder she more or less answered to Anon. Salmon . . . Anon . . . they could sound alike to a dog's ears.'

Isobel passed the magazine around us and we agreed that the markings were similar although not unique. 'There's a strong resemblance,' I said.

'Resemblance be damned,' Isobel said. 'It's the same bitch.'

Beth was at the sink, plucking tonight's dinner. 'You can't be sure,' she said.

Isobel disdained to reply. She could forget a face, an appointment or a good resolution but her memory for dogs was always phenomenal.

'Entered and handled by J. Franks,' she read out.

'If that's Johnny Franks,' I said, 'he's not Ayrshire. Dumfriesshire.'

'That's Ayrshire way,' Isobel retorted, 'which is what I said. Give him a ring. He'll know who he sold her to. Unless . . . '

I could guess what she meant. 'The body wasn't his,' I said. 'Johnny's about seven feet tall. The man we found was quite small. I'll phone Johnny after six.'

Isobel blew a raspberry. 'Don't be a cheapskate,' she said. 'Standard rate starts in a few minutes. Sergeant Ewell will be here soon, busting to know whether we've been able to help him. I'll feed the pups while Beth does some lunch. Henry can take over the plucking. You phone.'

On paper I was the senior partner, but Isobel had become a mother figure in the firm. Like any good mother she was indulgent, but when she put her foot down it was better to submit.

Directory Enquiries, I learned, had been computerised. In my innocence I would have thought that that would make it easier to hunt up a particular name in a

29

particular town, but no. Without the exact address, said the female voice, she was unable to help me. In the end I had to phone an acquaintance in the same Telecom area and ask him to look in his local phone-book.

I got Johnny Franks on the phone at last. He wanted to chat about old times at my expense, but I managed to bring him to the point. I can be extravagant about many things but something in my upbringing, during which the use of the telephone was considered to be a luxury and proof of a lack of forethought, makes me very conscious of the passing of the minutes while I am on the phone. 'We have Salmon of Glevedale here for the moment,' I said. 'What can you tell me about her history?'

A cheap little telephone amplifier lives beside the phone in the kitchen. It paid for itself in the first week in the time saved in not having to repeat telephone conversations for the benefit of partners who had heard only one end. I switched it on.

'She's one of a litter that we named after gamefish – Trout, Marlin, Grayling and so on. I sold her originally as a half-trained pup,' Johnny said in his deep bass voice. 'She had a marvellous pedigree and she was coming along well. The owner lived in a house called Glevedale, not far from here, hence the registered name. He finished her training for himself. Did a good job, mostly, but he came up against the usual steadiness problem. He didn't have access to a rabbit pen and instead of patience he used a check-lead and a stick; and you know the problems that can make.'

'By God I do!' I said.

'After that, even a fur glove would give her the shakes. He brought the bitch back to me for retraining and I said that I'd see what I could do. I even tried feeding her on top of madam's fur coat, which didn't do much for my love-life. In the end, I thought that I was making progress. In all other respects she was bloody good. I even ran her in a trial which was being held at Elmhill, on land which I knew for a fact was free of rabbits, but I'm damned if the only bunny for ten miles around wasn't shot under her nose. She was steady all right. Too damned steady. She didn't want to know about it and we were put out.' We heard him give a gusty sigh. 'Luck of the draw, I suppose, but it was hard. She was well worth an award.

'Her owner wanted to use her on a rough shoot which depended largely on the rabbits, so that was no good to him. I sold him a fully trained bitch and took Salmon back. I made him the best deal I could, because at least he'd been honest enough to admit that the fault was his. Even so, it was an expensive lesson for him.'

'It would be,' I said. I had had much the same experience more than once. 'But what happened to Salmon in the end?'

'An American turned up, last August, wanting a springer he could use while he was over here and then take back with him. Well, you know how it is at the start of the season. All the good dogs are sold, or if they're not you're in trouble. I only had my breeding stock, some pups and Salmon.

'As it turned out, she was just what he wanted. They don't shoot ground game in his neck of the woods and the last thing he wanted was a dog which would take off after a gopher or a squirrel. And he said that bum-punching quail over pointers was no more interesting than shooting clays down-the-line – the same going-away bird every time. I got a damned good price for her, for the second time. I'll take her back again if he's gone off her. Selling the same dog over and over again is my idea of good business.'

'You could change her name to Yoyo,' I said. 'It's

31

a better name than Salmon. Who was the American?'

'Hang on a moment.' I fretted on the line while he consulted his diary or his receipts book. 'His name was Falconer,' he said at last. 'David C. Falconer. I gathered that he was over here for the winter, setting up a UK branch of his business. I've no home address for him – the Kennel Club might be able to help – but he was staying at the Stoneleigh Hotel, near Kinross. That's a small place— '

'I know it,' I said. 'Thanks. If I can ever do you a favour . . . '

'You could lend me Salmon for a few days,' he suggested.

'Delighted,' I said, 'in return for the pick of all the litters.'

We exchanged insults for a minute in the way that only friends can and then rang off.

'If she's that good,' Beth said, 'I suppose we couldn't snatch a litter off her while she's here?'

It was a nice idea but, as I pointed out, we didn't have that marvellous pedigree; nor would we have clear title to the pups.

'Aren't you going to phone the Stoneleigh Hotel?' Isobel asked.

I switched off the amplifier. 'I ought to wait for the Sergeant,' I said reluctantly. I was as curious as the others. But I knew the Stoneleigh Hotel. It was, as Johnny had said, a small place but with sporting aspirations. The proprietor's brother was a wildfowling guide with control of the goose shooting on some of the land around Loch Leven. I had made use of his services in the past and sometimes referred my own clients to him. But the proprietor's wife was a very garrulous lady and our last phone-bill had been almost indistinguishable from the national debt.

'If you don't, I will,' Beth said.

I sighed and looked up the number. If those two spoke together, the call would never end.

As I feared, Mrs Blagdon answered the phone. She remembered me well and was disposed to be helpful. I switched on the amplifier again and asked for Mr Falconer.

'Gone, my dear,' she said. 'Home to the States. He left the Friday before last.'

That seemed to be that. 'Did he leave a forwarding address?' I asked.

My question released a spate of words which I was unable to stem.

'He was going to,' she said, 'but he never did. That's worried me, I don't mind telling you. I was expecting him to stay until the Saturday or Sunday, but on the Friday morning his room had been slept in but he'd gone and all his luggage with him. Well, he hadn't done a moonlight flit because his room was paid for until the weekend. He'd been with us since August and we'd given him a weekly rate. And the wee dog as well. As you know fine, we don't mind dogs in the rooms here, but his spaniel turned out to be a snorer so we'd made her a comfortable bed in the stables.

'I was surprised that he hadn't left a note or anything, or a tip for the maid, though some people are like that. And he had promised to leave a forwarding address.'

'Is there any mail for him?' I asked.

'Well, no. But I'll tell you something odd. Twice, when I was doing his room, I found in his waste basket an empty envelope which had come from the States, and each time it had been addressed to somebody else at General Delivery, Kinross, and marked "Collect". That's the same as Poste Restante, isn't it? If it had only been once I'd have thought that somebody'd given him a letter to read. But twice?'

33

At the risk of prolonging the call, I asked, 'Do you remember the names on the envelopes?'

'Yes. And that's another funny thing. The name was Hawker. Falconer, Hawker, it makes you think, doesn't it? And I'll tell you something else. There's been a policeman asking about him.'

That sounded as though the police already suspected the identity of the dead man. 'When was this?' I asked.

'In the middle of last week,' she said.

Not the same enquiry, then. 'The local police?' I asked.

'From Kirkcaldy, I think,' she said.

That told me nothing. The Fife Constabulary has its headquarters in Kirkcaldy. I was about to terminate the call with a quick but courteous enquiry after the state of her health, but the others were mouthing questions at me.

'What sort of man was he?' I asked reluctantly.

'Very brisk and businesslike and rather full of himself, not overly polite like most of those Yanks. But I could do with more like him. Always kept himself to himself and he was very considerate with the staff. And his wife was a real sweetie.'

'Wife?' I said. 'Was she staying with him?' Surely a wife would have reported a missing husband. Wives notice that sort of thing.

'She came over for a week in the early autumn. I think they'd had a quarrel and she came over to make it up. Very lovey-dovey they were for a while, but by the time she left they were bickering at each other again.'

There were many more questions which could have been asked but it seemed to me that I had already strayed into territory which the police would regard as their own. I thanked Mrs Blagdon and, with some difficulty, terminated the call.

34

'That clinches it,' Beth said. 'Anon's a snorer. Even from the isolation kennel she makes the windows rattle.'

'I don't want to say that I told you so,' Isobel said cheerfully, 'but I told you so.'

Henry's surplus leisure during his long retirement was filled by reading mysteries or watching them on the box, announcing the solution of each long before the dénouement, confidently although not always correctly. At the same time, Isobel was reluctant to let me claim the credit for her feat of recognition. They felt bound by good manners to signal their intention of leaving for home, but when Beth said that the pheasant would stretch to four portions they accepted with more haste than grace.

As it turned out, we had finished our meal and washed up and were at ease in the sitting room before Sergeant Ewell made his appearance. The Sergeant was not the sort of officer to be dealt with on the doorstep. I took him in, gave him a seat and offered him a drink.

'That would depend,' he said slowly. I noticed that he was looking tired. 'If you've nothing to tell me, I'll count myself as being off duty.'

'Perhaps you'd better stay on the wagon for a while,' I said.

I was about to reveal all, but Isobel jumped in ahead of me. 'What have they found out about the body?' she asked.

The Sergeant looked at her shrewdly. He knew perfectly well what she was really saying. We wanted his news first. 'I suppose there's no harm,' he said. 'You'll keep this in confidence?'

We said that we would.

'Mind, then, you've had nothing from me.' He leaned back in the deep chair and closed his eyes, only to re-open them suddenly. 'God, but it's good to sit down for a second. I was nearly away, then. We've been at panic-stations all day, and I was drawn into it over the dog.'

That could only mean one thing. 'You know who he was, then,' Henry said in tones of disappointment.

The Sergeant shook his head. Evidently there was an alternative meaning after all. 'It was the pathologist's report on the autopsy did it,' he said.

'Didn't he drown?' Isobel asked. I could tell that she was straining to keep the excitement out of her voice.

'He drowned. Oh, he was drowned all right. But he'd drowned in fresh water.'

'I always thought that he could have come down from upstream,' Henry said.

The Sergeant shook his head again. 'They thought that at first but now they say not. If he'd drowned in the river, they'd have found diatoms, whatever those may be, in the lungs or the heart. The pathologist said that if he'd had the body earlier he could have told where the water came from to within a mile, but now the most he can say for sure is that he suspects tap-water. Water that had been well filtered, anyway. And there were faint traces of what might have been soap or something suchlike. There was too little of it for a certain analysis.'

'That makes it murder,' Beth said, round-eyed. 'Doesn't it?'

'Aye. That's what they're thinking. It's hard to see how he could have drowned in the bath in all his shooting gear, gone down the plug-hole and come out in the Eden.' The Sergeant stopped and wiped the half-smile off his face. 'But that's not a fit subject for joking. It's all too easy to drown somebody in the bath. Think of George Joseph Smith. Just lift up the heels and the deed's half done for you. Now, I've told you all I know. Did you learn something from the dog?' He looked round our faces and must have detected suppressed triumph. 'You haven't?'

'Wrong for the second time,' Isobel said.

'The second time? I'm o'er tired for guessing games,' the Sergeant said.

'You were wrong first time,' Isobel said, 'when you told us that she was coming into season. She was going out. In fact, she's clear now. If she's been on the loose around St Andrews for the past ten days, God knows how many dogs have mounted her— '

'Who said anything about ten days?' the Sergeant asked. He was still relaxed and almost somnolent but it was clear that he was missing nothing.

Isobel and Henry looked at each other. 'That's how long it is since her owner vanished from his hotel,' Henry said.

We teased the Sergeant for a little longer and then gave him the facts. He wrote them down in his notebook. He seemed impassive but I could tell that we had rung a bell from the way his pencil checked at the name of the hotel and again at the presumed identity of the corpse.

Henry had not missed the signs. 'You knew of him?'

The Sergeant slapped his notebook shut. 'I've said too much already.'

'Nobody will know it from us,' Isobel said. 'And if you want to take all the credit, we won't contradict you. If it earns you your promotion, you can come back with a bottle of Champagne.'

He hesitated for a moment, evidently torn between duty and a desire not to seem ungracious. 'I'll tell you this much,' he said, 'and then I must get word through to Kirkcaldy. We were looking for the gentleman. His name was even mentioned in connection with the corpse, his build and weight being right, but only in a joking sort of a way. You see, we thought that he'd slipped out of the country.'

'Maybe he has,' I said. 'Maybe he passed the dog on to a friend before he left.'

'Maybe,' said the Sergeant. He seemed to have reached the limit of his revelations. He even refused to use our phone but hurried out to his car. From the window, we could see him speaking earnestly over his radio.

'Interesting,' Henry said. 'They thought that he'd left the country.'

'"Slipped out" was the expression,' I reminded him.

'So it was. Even more intriguing. The honest man leaves a trail behind him that a blind man could follow. But we already have two names for the gentleman and neither one of them rings true. Mark my words, Mr Falconer was up to no good.'

'When it comes to stating the obvious,' Isobel told her spouse, 'there's nobody to touch you.'

Three

On the Wednesday morning, the local paper pretended to be big with news although hard facts were few. It was stated, with apparent confidence, that the police were anxious to interview David Falconer, a citizen of the USA, in connection with the body found in the River Eden and 'other matters'. The statement was not attributed to a source in the police, but somebody had talked because the one fact revealed was that a spaniel, believed to have belonged to Mr Falconer, was being kept at Three Oaks Kennels awaiting a claimant.

The same morning brought a visit from another policeman, more senior than Sergeant Ewell and more self-assured. Chief Inspector Ainslie was young for his rank, very much the career policeman, brusque to the point of arrogance. His suit and overcoat were severe but tailor-made. He found the three partners and Henry washing dog-bowls and interviewed us on the spot.

His interest in the finding of the body was minimal. What he most wanted to know was about Anon – as we continued to call her. How certain was our identification? And where had she been worked?

We said that the identification was definite but that there was no way of knowing what ground she had worked on except that she seemed to be familiar with woodpigeon. A week or ten days adrift around St Andrews had obliterated any traces of soil or seeds. He wanted at first to take the spaniel away for forensic examination until Isobel pointed out that she had been thoroughly shampooed and de-infested. And no, there had been nothing about the sheep-ticks to suggest where she had picked them up. One sheep-tick was very like another and if you'd seen one you'd seen them all.

'You'd no business tampering with the dog,' he said at last in exasperation.

'Sergeant Ewell asked us to identify her,' Isobel said, 'not to preserve her in formalin.'

'Or have her stuffed,' I added. 'And we could hardly have left her as she was. We'd have had the RSPCA at us.'

'Sergeant Ewell should have taken her for forensic examination straight away.'

'They'd probably have killed her,' said Beth.

The Chief Inspector seemed unimpressed by that likelihood. He left at last, muttering about the wanton destruction of evidence.

The newspaper story brought several reporters to our door, each desperate to find some kind of a story to hang on the few facts available. I was about to let a photographer take a shot of Anon when I saw Henry, who had joined us for the morning and who was lurking in the background, shaking his head at me. I said that she was not giving any interviews and that if he cared to print a photograph of any passing springer we wouldn't contradict and the public would never know the difference.

I took Henry into the house and asked him what was bothering him. For once, Henry seemed uncertain. 'Buggered if I know,' he said. 'But that was no murder enquiry detective. He asked the wrong questions.'

'You think so?' I poured us some coffee while I wondered. 'His questions seemed reasonable to me. They want to know where the body was put in the water.'

'The body and the ground would tell them more about that,' Henry said. 'I've come round to your way of thinking. The body was dropped off the bridge. It's the one place you can take a car close to the water. They've no reason to believe that the dog got loose at the same place. If somebody was going to drown the dog, he wouldn't try it where people are sleeping not far away. I can think of a dozen questions that policeman didn't ask.'

'I can't think of any which haven't already been asked by others,' I said.

'But this chap came here specially to ask for clues as to where the dog might have been. And he wasn't particularly interested in the last ten days. He wanted to know all about what Mr Falconer had been up to before he was killed and he hoped that the dog could have told him where they'd been. If it had been part of a larger, murder enquiry, you'd have had two juniors here, not a senior man.'

I was unconvinced. In my experience, you got whoever was spare at the time. Seniority depended more on the newsworthiness and the spin-offs of the enquiry rather than on its importance.

My monthly masterclass, so-called, came round again that Sunday. It was an event which had grown insidiously out of nothing over a period of years until by now there was a surprising number of dog-owners prepared regularly to travel a distance and pay a fee in order to be put through exercises which they must by then have known by heart. For those, the event seemed to be as much social as practical. Others came once or twice and dropped out when some individual problem had been solved or pronounced insoluble.

The numbers attending seemed to vary from a peak early in the shooting season, when the results of the

41

long layoff were uncomfortably apparent, to drop off at the end of the season and then increase again slowly as young pups came into training for the season after next.

That winter, several litters of our pups had sold well and my class that Sunday was made up of eleven youngsters (eight of them from Three Oaks stock) plus one adult dog, a newcomer. This last was a remarkable animal, with a nose as long as that of a Shetland collie. His colour was neither the yellow of a Labrador nor the dark red of a setter but something in between, almost an orange and so bright that I could imagine it glowing in the dark. His owner, a thin, red-haired man with a blue chin, horn-rimmed glasses and an anxious manner, assured anyone who would listen that the dog was at least half Labrador, provoking much speculation among the class, whenever the proud owner was out of earshot, as to just what on earth the other half could have been. The Saluki was mentioned more than once, although it was clear that, unless the product was a freak or 'sport', at least one other grandparent had to have been involved. A sweepstake would have been held if there had been any way of settling the question.

I was also assured that the dog was an excellent retriever, very good at finding lost game, responsive to the spoken word or to hand signals but absolutely deaf to the whistle. There seemed to be nothing wrong with the dog's hearing so I took a look at the owner's whistle. Beth took the two of them away with a few dummies and a pocketful of edible rewards, for a series of exercises of gradually increasing difficulty, while I tried to impress the puppy-owners with the need to make haste very, very slowly.

A custom had grown up, and one which I had done little to discourage, whereby I was invited to lunch at the hotel as the guest of those who intended to eat there. I often delegated this pleasant duty to Beth, but on this occasion she preferred to stay and oversee one of our brood bitches who had run her time, although the bitch was perfectly capable of managing alone and Isobel had an uncanny instinct which always brought her to the kennels as whelping began. I was carried off to the hotel by two of the pup-owners. These were a brace of almost identical ladies, big-busted and blue-rinsed with loud voices and similar tweeds, whose husbands were already waiting in the bar. I had come to know all four over the previous winter.

The man with the orange retriever decided at the last moment to join us. His name, I had learnt from the dog's inoculation certificate, was McConnelly and he was understood to be a civil servant. Why he attended the lunch was a mystery. He was a teetotaller, he lived less than an hour away, and because of a grumbling ulcer he limited himself to a small selection of the blandest foods.

The two ladies, who were evidently also the drivers, were equally abstemious; but their husbands had been idling away a couple of hours in the bar. One of them, a tall man whose bald head was compensated for by a huge moustache, was the first to drag the conversation, which was dog-oriented, away from the general and towards the particular.

'You had an eventful wildfowling trip last week,' he said.

'A body!' said the lady who I think was his wife. I never was quite sure who was married to whom. 'I'm sure I'd have made an exhibition of myself.'

My mind refused to come up with a suitably inoffensive answer so I held my peace.

'Have they identified him yet?' the man with the moustache asked.

'Not for sure, as far as I know,' I said cautiously.

43

Sergeant Ewell had not exactly sworn me to secrecy but I had a feeling that a little discretion would be appreciated. 'The police aren't telling me anything.'

'According to the local rag,' said the man with the moustache, 'they want to interview somebody called Falconer. My guess was that that's who they thought the body was.'

'But wasn't there something about a dog?' the other husband asked. He was stout and tweedy and smelled of gin and aftershave.

'They found a springer bitch which had been on the loose around St Andrews for a week or two,' I said. That much had been in the papers. 'There's no easy way to tell whether she had belonged to the dead man.'

'A dead wildfowler without a dog and a loose gundog without an owner, in the same area at the same time,' one of the ladies said thoughtfully. 'That would be stretching coincidence a bit far, wouldn't it?'

'Stranger things happen,' Mr McConnelly said, looking up for the first time through his heavy spectacles.

'That's true,' said the man with the moustache. 'They'd have a hell of a job proving the identity of a dog. I've always said that we ought to tattoo a number inside the ear or something. A trained dog costs a lot of money.'

'But tissue-typing would work on a dog, wouldn't it?' said the other husband. 'Genetic fingerprinting, they call it.'

As it happened, I knew something about the genetic fingerprinting of dogs; indeed, I had nearly had to resort to it the year before in a dispute over Jason's ownership. 'If her sire and dam are still alive,' I said, 'or if they could trace other offspring from the same pair, they could prove that she had come from one of those joint litters. Unless they could account for every other pup from those matings, I think that that's as far as they could go.'

'They can do it from hair, can't they?' said the man with the moustache. 'I mean, if they had some hair from the basket they think the bitch came from they could prove that the bitch they'd found was the same one. Couldn't they?'

'Wouldn't help much if they couldn't prove a connection with the dead man,' said the other husband. He had taken aboard a good few drinks but his mind was still working. 'Not as a help to proving the man's death for probate purposes, I mean.' He paused, took a sip of his red wine and chuckled. Unfortunately he tried to do both at the same time. One of the ladies – possibly his wife – dabbed at him with a napkin and the conversation was side-tracked into the staining properties of Rhône wines for a minute or two.

'What I was thinking,' he resumed at last, 'was this. Imagine that he was murdered. Imagine that his murderer also had a springer bitch and she'd run off while he was dumping the body. The murderer ends up with the dead man's dog. Rather than attract attention, he leaves matters as they are. The possibilities for confusion are endless.'

'You read too many of those detective stories,' said the woman who I thought wasn't his wife.

'Maybe. But can't you imagine a murderer combing out some other springer bitch and sprinkling the hairs over the dead man's dog-basket?'

I stopped listening. I had quite enough problems to solve without wasting mental effort on hypotheses which were as muddled as they were fanciful.

Beth pounced on me as soon as I got back to Three Oaks. She knew a great deal about dog training but was always keen to learn more. 'How did you work the magic on that man's dog?' she demanded. 'You sent us off to do some exercises which had no business making any difference; and when we came to using the whistle the dog hesitated once and then got it right every time.'

I thought of testing her but decided to be kind. 'He was embarrassed enough, showing his mutt among all the pedigree dogs,' I said. 'I wanted to spare his blushes. If he wants a proper dog next time around he may come back to us.'

'But how did you *do* it?'

'Very simple,' I said. 'You noticed what kind of whistle it was?'

'One of the silent whistles,' she said. 'When you gave it back to him, you'd screwed the barrel out so that its pitch had come down to within human hearing. But that wouldn't make any difference to a dog.'

'I also gave it a poke through while he wasn't looking. It was the silentest whistle you didn't ever hear. It was bunged up with a hardened mixture of spit, pocket fluff and the sort of detritus which seems to collect in the pockets of shooting men.'

Beth had often cleaned out my pockets. 'Bits of pigeon feather and rape-seeds. And I thought you'd done something clever,' she said disgustedly.

As the man with the moustache had said, trained gun-dogs are valuable assets. Even more so is a breeding strain with a successful record in field trials. I was sometimes both amazed and relieved that people came to our door prepared to pay our prices, but when feed and time and stud fees were taken into account, not to mention our investment in kennels and runs, those prices represented only a modest profit margin. The shrinking of the keepering profession had removed some of the sternest competition.

We had had our troubles. Any business which is highly competitive and which touches on matters which some consider to be contentious can expect occasional attempts at theft or sabotage.

Our original, rather primitive security system had so far averted any serious losses. This was based on the fact that, while electronic detectors respond to any passing bird, the dogs themselves soon learn to be a more selective alarm-system. The kennels were set at a distance from the house which was itself relatively soundproof, so a system of hidden microphones relayed any night-noises to loudspeakers in the house. False alarms were sometimes caused by prowling foxes or by stray dogs attracted to the scent of a bitch in season, but in general the system had worked so well that we had never seen fit to replace it but had merely extended it by fitting each kennel with a padlock. The multiplicity of keys which ordinary locks would have entailed was not to be contemplated, so we had settled for combination padlocks of the type sold for bicycles, all set to the same combination.

That same Sunday night, a tumult of barking over the loudspeakers dragged me, if not out of my sleep, at least somewhere close to the surface where consciousness begins. I wrapped sleep around my mind, hoping against hope that whatever was making all the noise would go away.

Beth dug me in the ribs with her elbow. 'The dogs are barking,' she said.

I had been in the middle of a dream about walking the dogs until my feet were sore, so naturally I took both the barking and her comment to be part of that dream and snuggled down. But she was made of sterner stuff. She elbowed me again.

'We've got an intruder,' she said loudly and clearly.

I came to the surface and stayed there or thereabouts. 'Probably only a fox,' I said, with much less clarity.

She managed to extract a meaning from my mumble.

'That isn't the way they bark at a fox,' she said. 'It isn't "keep away" barking. It's more like "I don't like this game at all" barking. Get up and do something.'

Without quite relinquishing my hold on sleep, I got out of bed and tottered towards where I remembered having seen the window. The night was dark, but in daylight most of the kennels and their runs were visible away to the right. Near where I knew them to be, somebody was messing about with a torch.

Suddenly, I was fully awake. 'We've got an intruder,' I said.

'That's what— '

'I'm going out,' I said. I let the heavy curtains fall back into place, groped my way back to the bed and switched on the bedside lamp. 'You call the cops.'

I grabbed for my slippers and dressing-gown, discarded them again and began to drag on whatever clothing came to hand. The heating was off and the cool of the room reminded me that it was still February outside. I was not going to freeze for any intruder. I could hear Beth gabbling into the phone as I felt my way downstairs. Rather than give warning to the intruders I groped around in the dark. By the time I had found my own torch and a pair of shoes Beth was at my side again, dressed as for an Arctic expedition.

'It doesn't need both of us,' I said.

'It might. Anyway, I'm not being left in here on my own.'

I decided that I had no wish to be alone in the dark and cold either, so I gave a grunt which she could take for reluctant acquiescence and opened the front door.

The torchlight seemed to have vanished. Darkness was almost total but I knew every inch of the ground and two of the dogs – Samson and Moonbeam from their voices – were still barking. I ran in that direction over wet grass, hoping to hell that nobody had left a wheelbarrow in the way.

The barks were subsiding. Evidently the dogs had decided that the emergency was over. I was less certain. Rather than collide in the dark with an intruder who had heard me coming, I switched on the torch and found that I had covered more ground than I thought and was about to bump into the wire of the isolation kennel. I pulled up and Beth ran into my back.

'There's nobody here now,' she said. 'But look!' She took my hand and steadied the beam of the torch.

I looked. A hole had been clipped in the heavy wire of the run and Anon seemed to have vanished. The motherly bitch we had put in with her was sitting wide-eyed in the run, obviously wondering what was meant by these unfamiliar events in the night.

If the intruder had been after one particular bitch, it would have taken him time to identify Anon and more time to fiddle with the combination padlock before giving up and beginning to cut the wire. If he was making for a car, we could not be far behind. If he was heading across country, we had lost him.

I turned towards the gates and at that moment the yelp of a dog came from somewhere in the road. I oriented myself, switched off the torch and ran. Behind me, I heard Beth fall over something.

The night had seemed pitch dark, but my eyes were adjusting and there was faint starlight. I stopped at the gates, looked around and listened. Two miles away a disgruntled pair of headlights swept along the main road. Further off, I could make out the blinking of a blue lamp and the yodel of a police klaxon reached through the silent air. Beth's phone-call was producing prompt results or somebody else had troubles.

Not far to my right, a darker mass, a vehicle, came

into focus against the dark strip of the road. Near it, something was moving.

The obvious and sensible action was to stand back and use the torch to see faces and read the car's number-plate. That was what Beth told me later, more than once. Instead, I ran towards the movement, switching on the torch at the last moment.

A dog bolted under my feet, nearly bringing me down. The thief had lost his booty, but I was already committed.

If I ever looked at the car or van, it failed to register. As I recovered my balance, the torch showed me a figure, presumably male, in dark clothing. Something swung, glinting, from his left hand which might have been a chain dog-lead. I dropped the torch and plunged forward, angry at the intrusion and the theft but most of all at being woken up. It came to me, too late, that there had been another glint in his right hand.

My old training in unarmed combat was still with me, but my instructor had never prepared me for an encounter in the dark with an opponent who had a knife in one hand and a chain in the other. Something lashed me across the face and as I dropped one hand to parry a knife in the gut he switched to an overarm stab. My other hand caught him in the face but at the same moment something burned into my left shoulder.

I went down with the shock of it although there was no pain yet. I had time to hope that he had missed the carotid artery. Then a boot connected with my face. My head bounced off the road and I blacked out.

Four

I came round, slowly and painfully, alone in a single-bed ward. There was no need to ask where I was; I had occupied that bed before. Outside the large window, dark clouds were swirling ponderously across a lighter sky. I seemed to be on a drip and my left arm was immobilised. My shoulder was on fire, the parts of my face did not seem to fit together and the lump on the back of my head made the pillow feel like concrete. I was weaker than any kitten and, when I tried to move, my head swam.

Yet, underlying all those discomforts, there was a feeling that alertness and wellbeing were lurking not too far beyond my reach. I recognised that feeling immediately. I had felt the same symptoms of recovery during my long illness, whenever the frequent blood transfusions had renewed my depleted corpuscles. Somebody else's blood was doing a grand job in my veins.

The electronics to which I was attached must have registered my awakening, because a nurse came in to take a look at me. She fetched a doctor who took a closer look and expressed qualified satisfaction. The knife, he said, had missed the main artery but had severed a lesser blood vessel and done some damage to the muscle. I was more concerned about my face but again he was reassuring. I might look for the moment like something in Frankenstein's worst dream, he said, but my beauty was not ruined for ever. In a month or two, Beth would be able to look at me without a shudder.

The police must have been short-handed. There was no constable waiting at my bedside. But the nurse made a phone-call and Sergeant Ewell, neat as ever, showed up half an hour later and tutted sympathetically over my state. Beth had already given him the gist of the story – several times, I gathered, and in tones of mounting indignation. Beth was always inclined to repeat herself in periods of crisis. I filled in the details of my battle with the intruder. He pressed me to say whether the man, or his car, had been large or small, dark or light.

'I wasn't looking at his blasted car,' I said. 'I was trying to watch his hands. And he had something over his head – a balaclava or a ski-mask or the traditional stocking, I suppose.'

'You must have gained an impression. Was he fat or thin?'

I tried to think back although my wits were still addled. 'He seemed broad,' I said at last, 'but that might have been the effect of loose clothing.' There was something else but whatever it was kept slipping away out of my reach.

The Sergeant changed his ground. 'Would you jalouse,' he said, 'that your caller was after that particular dog? The wee bitch that belonged to the dead man?'

'Guessing's your business,' I said, 'not mine.'

'We deduce,' he said reprovingly. 'We never guess.'

'So you want me to do your guessing for you? If he was a thief, an unidentified bitch wouldn't be much use to him. Even if he knew her identity and had the pedigree he couldn't use a stolen dog for breeding. Logically, he had to be after Anon. But people aren't logical. He could be some nutter who wanted a pet or a gundog.'

52

The Sergeant said umhumm, or words to that effect, and asked whether I had any ideas as to why somebody might want Anon in particular.

'Unless some idiot was attracted by the newspaper accounts, I haven't the least idea,' I said. The Sergeant looked dashed. 'Are you still hoping to solve the mystery single-handed?' I asked him. 'Didn't the identification of the body give you enough of a boost?'

He had the grace to look abashed. 'You did me some good,' he admitted. 'One more like that might just do the trick.'

'Don't count on me,' I told him.

Sergeant Ewell made it clear that he had expected more from me. He left and the nurse took over. I was fed, washed and emptied with dispassionate precision and left in a state fit to be seen by another visitor.

This turned out to be Henry, as tall and worn and lively as ever. I looked past him but there was no sign of Beth and I suddenly realised that I had little or no idea what had happened after I was knocked out.

'Is Beth all right?' I asked him.

He looked at me curiously. 'She's well. The question is whether you approximate to the same condition.'

'I'm fine,' I said. But despite my brave words I must still have been in an emotional state, because I could think of only one other explanation for her absence. 'Doesn't she care?' I asked shrilly.

Henry made soothing gestures. 'Of course she cares,' he said. 'She cares too much. Every time your name comes up she starts weeping again. Isobel told me to come and see how you were before we let her visit. At least we can prepare her for the shock.' That news would have been comforting but Henry spoiled the effect. 'Anyway,' he said, 'they're both busy. Starlight's on the point of whelping and you aren't there to keep things going. I've tried to help when I could.'

That, although humbling, made sense. Our living depended on the litters; and the health and fecundity of one of our best brood bitches was not to be neglected. 'Ask her to come and see me when she has time,' I said.

Henry seated himself carefully in the one chair, deposited a paper bag of assorted fruit on the locker and studied me with interest. 'The way you look just now,' he said at last, 'you're hardly a reassuring spectacle to greet a young bride. How do you feel?'

'It depends who I'm feeling,' I said. 'Don't be daft, Henry. I feel bloody awful.'

'You look as though you might. Did you know that you've got the marks of a chain across the lump on your face?'

'I didn't,' I said. 'They've been keeping mirrors out of my reach. But I believe you. I think he had a chain dog-lead. That would explain something. You know how a chain slip-lead can come off over a dog's head if it falls slack.' I broke off on another thought. 'Did we get Anon back?'

'You did,' he said. 'Beth seems to have behaved with remarkable common sense. More so, I may say, than yourself. You'd left her behind in the dark. She heard the car drive off – it sounded a bit of a rattletrap, she says – so she headed in that direction. She stumbled across you and found your torch and she stayed with you, maintaining pressure on your wound, until the police showed up and radioed for an ambulance. She gave them a quick statement and then did a tour, whistling and calling for Anon – who turned up again not far from the house. Then and only then did Beth phone us, enlist our aid and comfort and allow herself the luxury of a good cry.

'Anon, I may add, is none the worse and, at Sergeant Ewell's request, has been transferred to a boarding kennel some miles away and under a different name.'

'The Sergeant was here about half an hour ago, but he never told me that. I wonder why.' As I spoke the answer came to me. 'If somebody wants Anon and doesn't know that she's been removed, there may be more visitors. Henry— '

'Calm down,' he said. 'Isobel and I have moved in with Beth for the moment. The Sergeant is keeping as much of an eye on the place as he can manage and if there are any more noises in the night we're to phone him, at his home if need be, and not to go outside until he gets there.'

I relaxed again. 'My brain isn't working properly yet,' I said. 'I can't think why the hell anybody would want to steal Anon.'

Henry waggled his shaggy eyebrows at me. 'My brain, on the other hand, is working perfectly,' he said, 'and I can't think of a reason either. We're beginning to sound like our womenfolk,' he added. 'Until Starlight started to pup, they were beating their brains out, and mine, on the subject. In fact, they only had two topics of conversation – that and your prospects of surviving.'

'Did they come to any conclusions?'

'Certainly not that you were going to make it back to health. They had you relapsed, wheelchair-bound, brain-damaged and contracting Aids from the blood transfusions – despite all the reassurances from the doctors,' Henry added hastily in case I should be taking him seriously. 'Nor about Anon. Even if she belonged to the dead man, and even if she witnessed his demise, she hardly constitutes an incriminating witness. Dogs, after all, take likes or dislikes to people for reasons which our atrophied senses can't perceive, so that a growl or a fawn, or even a bite, would hardly be evidence of anything other than an unfamiliar aftershave, an inadvertent threat expressed in some obscure aspect

55

of body language or even the smell of a fox or weasel tracked in from the garden.'

The point seemed to be a good one, yet there surely had to be a reason somewhere. 'You're sure that Beth recovered the same bitch?' I asked. 'It wasn't a clever substitution?'

'They both seemed satisfied. All three, if you count the bitch.'

'It was a silly idea,' I admitted.

'Not half so silly as some of the birdbrained theories those two have been bandying around. Before Anon's transfer elsewhere, Isobel examined her for implants and got quite peevish when I enquired whether she suspected that Anon was carrying secret microphones on behalf of a foreign power; and Beth went over her, hair by hair, in the hope that she had been tattooed with a secret map or message and her coat then allowed to grow back over it again. Apart from a few of the scars which any shooting dog collects, and the fact that she seems to be pregnant after her time on the loose among the randy tykes in St Andrews, she's in more or less mint condition.'

We pondered in silence. 'Damned if I know,' I said at last. 'It isn't as if the presumed owner was alive to pay a reward.'

'Or a ransom.' Henry stretched his long legs and tried to settle himself more comfortably in the hard chair. 'And even if he were still among those present, he doesn't seem to have been the sort of man who would part with good cash for the sake of a dog. Quite a lot of facts have been emerging about him. There was a whole screed about him in yesterday's paper.'

I thought back. Had my injuries left me with a memory gap? 'I don't remember that,' I said.

'You wouldn't,' Henry said. He hummed and hawed for a while and then said, 'I suppose it's all right to tell you. This is Tuesday. You've lost a day, in surgery and under sedation. I'll bring you the cutting, if you like.'

'Tell me.'

'You're not too tired?'

'From bitter experience,' I said, 'I'm going to be bored out of my skull. And I won't be able to sleep with bits of me hurting like hell and while I'm lying idle in a strange bed. There's a lump in the mattress which feels exactly like a dead baby. For God's sake give me something else to think about.'

'If you're sure,' he said doubtfully. 'At least your tongue seems to have recovered its cutting edge. They've identified him as a much wanted American con artist. As it happens, I can fill in a bit more of the financial background than was known to the reporter on the local rag.' (Henry had once been a power among the financial institutions and even in his long retirement had made a point of keeping up with news from the world's markets.) 'Also, Sergeant Ewell was in a chatty mood. You may not know it, but since the Savings and Loan business in America was deregulated, that sphere of operations has become a public scandal. Millions of dollars have been pouring through that market and it's only too easy for an unscrupulous management to siphon off large wads of it. The method most often favoured is for one member to buy a parcel of cheap land for development. Then they sell it from one to the other at a heavy mark-up. I've heard of the same parcel of land changing hands as often as twenty or thirty times in a single day. Then, when they reckon they've squeezed all the juice out of the fruit, the company buys the land and a hotel or a supermarket gets built, all with the investors' money. The investors are allowed to see a small profit, but nothing like what they were entitled to.

'But our late friend – he seems to have been known

as Peregrine at that time – was reluctant either to wait or to share. He went through the motions of setting up a legitimate Savings and Loan company and then, working alone from a rented office, he placed some impressive advertisements, stating that his company would pay one per cent above the going rate. Money came pouring in. He made some conspicuous but low-cost speculations, paid some interest out of capital and then chose the optimum moment to grab the money and run.

'They've been looking for him, and even more intently for the money, all over the States; but like the Snark (or was it the Boojum?) he had "swiftly and suddenly vanished away as though he had never been there". They still don't even know his real identity.'

'I don't think it was either of them,' I said.

'Either of who?'

'The snark, or— '

Henry glared at me. 'For God's sake!' he said. 'Do you want to hear the story or don't you?'

'Go on,' I said. 'But do try to get the facts right.'

'Pick one more nit and I'll leave you wondering,' Henry said. 'When our police contacted the FBI, looking for help in identifying a corpse, presumed to be American, with a faked passport and a certain description, some bright lad noticed the falconry theme running through the names and sent over a set of fingerprints and an Indentikit. The Identikit was instantly recognised by Mrs Thingummy at the Stoneleigh Hotel. The fingertips of the body only yielded some inadequate fragments of prints, but the fingerprints from America turned up again in a hired car parked on the golf course in St Andrews. Nobody had bothered about it until the hirer became anxious because a rental payment was overdue.'

If I failed to sleep now, it would be from having too much rather than too little to think about. 'If he was pulling a scam over here,' I said, 'that could well explain why he was knocked off.'

'He was and it could,' Henry said, 'although it seems that the biggest loser is probably the British taxpayer. Our Mr Falconer must have realised that he had made the States a little too hot for himself. So he came over with a load of faked documentation, ostensibly to set up a factory making computer hardware for the oil industry. His references, although spurious, were good and he was welcomed with open arms. He rented space near Glenrothes, hired a few staff, obtained every grant and loan available and all the credit which could be arranged, ordered and re-sold some very expensive equipment, took deposits against orders and is believed to have converted the whole lot into cash.'

'Which has disappeared?'

'Which, as you say, has mysteriously disappeared. It's to be presumed that he intended to do the same, although not in the manner which eventuated.'

'So whoever knocked him off scooped the pool?' I suggested.

Henry pulled a face indicative of uncertainty. 'That doesn't necessarily follow, although one would suppose so. Reading between the lines, they must suspect that he had some help over here; he found his way too smoothly through the morass of red tape to have been an ignorant Yankee making a raid. And he must have planned his vanishing act for roughly when it happened, because all personal mail stopped dead.

'According to the press – who do, for once, seem to have been making a token gesture in the direction of accuracy – Mrs – um— '

'Blagdon,' I said.

'Thank you. Mrs Blagdon at the hotel says that he had a friend in these parts. They never saw the friend or heard his name, but she knows that they spent some time roughshooting or wildfowling together. And because the friend hasn't come forward it's a fair guess that he was implicated.'

'What about the wife?' I said. 'I suppose that she really was his wife?'

'Who knows? She came, she went.'

I had a host of questions to ask but another nurse entered at that moment and made shooing noises at Henry. 'You were only supposed to stay for five minutes,' she said. 'You were only allowed in at all because you promised not to excite the patient.'

Henry left and the nurse started to do some of the more personal things that nurses do to patients. 'So it's all right for you to excite me?' I said. 'But not Henry?'

She gave me a playful slap across the backside and left me to my thoughts. So there was a large sum of money adrift, probably in the hands of the murdering associate but quite possibly not. Mr Falconer might have concealed the money before his unkind friend drowned him in the bathtub. Suppose, I thought, just suppose that the cash had been translated into something small but precious, such as one large diamond, which had then been implanted into the spaniel ready for shipment back to the States.

But no, I told myself. I had faith in my partners. Isobel had looked for signs of an implant. And Beth, in her hair by hair examination, would not have missed the signs of recent surgery.

Would she?

It helped to keep my mind off my discomforts. I wove fantasies around the subject until I fell asleep again.

They kept me in hospital for ten dull and humiliating days. I make a bad patient, despite having had a great deal of practice. I would have rebelled sooner, except that March was indeed coming in like the proverbial lion. Wind and rain were lashing the ward window. Confinement at home would be as bad. Beth, I knew, would be rushed off her feet in that weather, with an army of spaniels to dry after exercise or training. Caring for an invalid might be the last straw.

Beth came to see me whenever she could – emotional at first, competent always, but harassed much of the time. One of the dogs brought in for retraining had imported pediculosis, an outbreak of the lice to which spaniel puppies are particularly susceptible. Henry came more often and kept me up to date with the lack of progress which the police were making. He had been pressed into service as assistant delouser and was glad of an excuse to escape now and again.

On the eleventh day I awoke to a beautiful morning. A change of hue had washed over the visible countryside, delicate as a maiden's blush, suggesting that spring was beginning to stir. I was already known as an unwelcome guest and when I set my mind to making a real nuisance of myself the authorities seemed relieved to remove my stitches and allow me home. I was released only after dire warnings about taking it easy, not exerting myself and above all not to put any strain on my shoulder.

The warnings were unnecessary. I tired easily and my left arm was unusable. I felt awkward and guilty, sitting around while the others laboured, but Beth and Isobel soon decided that my assistance was more trouble than it was worth.

Beth put it in a nutshell. 'Go away,' she said tiredly. 'I don't have *time* to be helped.'

So I was banished to the sitting room, or to a seat on the grass when the sun shone, to assist with the paperwork, teach the older puppies some elementary retrieving with tennis balls from my armchair and deal with visitors. Business always turns brisk when you are worst equipped to cope with it. During the next fortnight I sold two trained dogs and seven or eight young puppies, accepted several dogs for board and training and dished out free advice to anybody who came seeking it. The role of guru was still a novelty to me and I suppose that I pontificated. It paid off. I had time to give the purchasers of trained dogs much more than my usual brief lecture on words of command and how to accustom the dog to a new handler. One of those pairs is still gaining honours in field trials.

Murder and GBH would have seemed very far away, except that among the visitors were several reporters. They tried to make a sensation out of my story but, apart from the events already being stale, there was little drama in the coincidence of a man who had found a body being the victim of an attack. They never came back and the story never rated more than a line or two.

Another visitor was a young woman, very thin except for large hips unflattered by yellow stretch slacks. She seemed to be the nervous type, which probably accounted for her lack of flesh. She could have been pretty if her teeth had been straightened. Her voice was prissy but her accent was good.

It had turned showery again, so I saw her in the sitting room. She was to be married later in the year, she told me with a flash of a modest engagement ring and, her fiancé being a shooting man, she was thinking of giving him a springer as a wedding present. Whenever her approaching wedding was mentioned she turned red and twined her fingers together.

We talked money. The price of a good pup made her blink but she said that she could manage it. The cost of a trained dog is strictly for the well-heeled or the fanatic and was quite beyond her means.

'You see, I'm out of a job now. I worked for Atlantis

62

Controls,' she added, with the air of one dropping a famous name. When I failed to react, she added, 'The firm which just went bust. The boss turned up dead. The papers said that you found the body, so when I thought about a spaniel for a wedding present yours was the one name I knew.'

'Not a very good basis on which to choose a strain of gundog,' I said.

'No,' she said, laughing. Laughter would have made her almost beautiful except that it showed off those uneven teeth and brought on another fit of finger-twining. 'But, to be fair to myself, I did make some enquiries and heard nothing but good. Which is better than you can say about poor Mr Falconer. The names they're calling him!' She looked at me earnestly. 'I can hardly believe that he was what they say he was. He seemed so . . . nice.' The hesitation was excessive for choosing just the wrong word.

I refrained from mentioning that seeming nice is the stock-in-trade of every rogue. 'You worked closely with him?' I asked her.

'I was his private secretary. Nobody gets to know a man better, except perhaps a wife. And if he was a crook he certainly fooled me. I did all his correspondence and it seemed perfectly above board.'

She was beginning to revive my flagging curiosity. 'You mentioned a wife,' I said. 'I heard that his wife came over to stay with him for a week or so. Did you meet her?'

For some reason, she hesitated again before answering. I guessed that there had been some jealousy between the privileged wife and the trusted secretary. 'No,' she said at last. 'But he told me that she fell in love with his dog. I could understand that, she's adorable. That's another reason why I decided to come to you. If she's still here . . . do you think that I could buy Salmon?'

63

'She isn't here,' I said. 'She's been moved. You'd better have a word with the police. Our local Sergeant would help you if he could. Tell me, did you ever meet the shooting friend he's supposed to have spent time with?'

'I think so, once.' She had recovered from her initial nervousness and was speaking more confidently. 'He was a tall man with sandy hair. Oh, and he had a slight limp. Mostly he was just a voice on the phone to me. Rather a deep voice with a trace of Glasgow in it. But I don't think that they spent all that much time together, just early morning visits to the shore. Mr Falconer sometimes brought back a duck for me. But he had other places to go and shoot. He got to know some of the local farmers. And every few weeks he'd have me phone and book a place – a Gun, he called it – on one of the big, commercial shoots.'

'Did you never hear the friend's name?'

'Only the first time. After that, whenever I heard the voice I'd put him through. I've tried and tried to remember the name and I've been over it with the police. It began with a J but what it was I just don't remember.' She broke off and changed to a pleading, little-girl voice. 'Couldn't you tell me where Salmon of Glevedale is now? Perhaps if I spoke to them . . . '

'The police took her away,' I said. 'They'll be holding on to her in case the widow turns up to claim her. I think you'd do better to forget it.'

We seemed to have run out of topics. She said that she'd think about a pup, really she would. As I showed her to the door, I remembered to ask her name.

'McGillivray,' she said. She thanked me excessively for what, on my part, had been no more than a normal sales-talk.

★ ★ ★

Sergeant Ewell arrived not long afterwards on the pretext of examining, under the new legislation, my gunsafe. He had seen this many times before, so I guessed that he was looking for coffee, a chat and any more hints which he could use to further his own chances of promotion. Beth brought the coffee and joined us. She sat near where Miss McGillivray had sat, looking youthful and delicious by contrast.

Beth asked how the investigation was going.

'They're looking gey hard at the banking fraternity,' the Sergeant said. 'It's thought that any fool with a wee bit understanding of accountancy could follow the ins and outs of the industrial grants, but the money vanished so cleanly and with so little trace that they think he must have had help from inside a bank. There's no sign of a cheque, a withdrawal slip, or a statement even.'

'There's a lot of people in banking,' I said.

'No doubt of that. Lothian and Borders aren't happy about it, being asked to check up on the Edinburgh banking men over a murder committed in Fife. And with so little to go on.'

'They'll be limiting themselves to the holders of shotgun certificates,' I said. 'That should cut it down a bit.'

'Likely so,' said the Sergeant. 'But that alone takes an age of checking.' My comment reminded him of something else. 'There's been a shotgun found in the Eden. A twelve-bore. It had silted over but one of the horse-riders kicked it up again at low tide. It's awful rusty, I'm told, after that time in salt water, but they can tell it's a Browning. That's American, isn't it?'

'Belgian,' I said. 'But if it's recent it was probably made in Japan. John Moses Browning was an American but he emigrated to Belgium. A lot of Browning shotguns go to America, but they come here as well. I suppose it was found just to the east of Coble Shore?'

'Aye, it was. How did you know that?' The Sergeant's voice was bland and he seemed relaxed and at home in his usual chair, but his eyes were fixed on mine.

'That's where it would be,' I said. 'But it could just as easily have been lost by a genuine fowler. I can imagine a man laying his gun down to deal with a goose or a duck which is winged and still struggling. In the dark, he can't find his gun again and the tide's coming in fast.'

'But if his murderer was getting rid of the dead man's gun?'

'There would always be the risk that it would turn up again,' I said. 'The easiest place to get to would be just above the bridge, though it's not the kind of place a man could be cut off by the tide and drowned. But he could drive a car to the small car park by Coble Shore, walk across the spit from the Reserve side and as far out on the sand as the tide would let him. If the gun turned up there, that would at least be consistent with an accidental drowning.'

The Sergeant thought about it, nodding slowly. Something else was causing an itch at the back of my mind. 'Can you tell me the name of Falconer's secretary?' I asked him.

'McGillivray,' he said. 'They've given her a clean bill of health.' I was about to change subjects when he went on, 'A rather scatterbrained old maid or she'd have seen that something was up.' He looked into my face again. 'What's adae?'

'I asked because there was a young woman here just before you came. She said that her name was McGillivray and that she'd been his secretary; but there was something about her manner which didn't quite ring true. For one thing, she was twitching with nerves. I wouldn't have called her an old maid. She was very interested to know where the springer bitch had gone.'

66

'A young woman?' He took out his notebook. 'What description?'

'Red-brown hair,' I said, 'with a wave which looked natural but probably wasn't. Oval face, good skin, slightly pinched nose and crooked teeth. She was self-conscious about her teeth so she tried not to part her lips when she talked or smiled. Generally skinny but big around the hips. Medium height.'

'Age,' he asked, writing busily.

I shrugged. I never was good at women's ages. 'Thirty-ish,' I suggested.

'I saw her going in,' Beth said. 'You didn't mention that she had sexy legs.'

'I didn't notice,' I said. (Beth looked disbelieving.) 'She said – and I pass this on for what it's worth – that Mr Falconer's shooting friend was a tall man, fair-haired and with a limp. Voice deep and with a slight Glasgow accent.'

The Sergeant made a careful note. 'Did either of you happen to notice her car?' he asked.

I shook my head. Beth said, 'I think she walked up from the road.'

The Sergeant smiled sadly. 'Just my luck,' he said. 'I'll pass along both descriptions and if anybody turns up answering your description of her she'll have some difficult questions to answer.'

'She'll probably just say that she saw the chance of a cheap dog,' Beth said.

'She can have her as far as I'm concerned,' said the Sergeant. 'Really, that spaniel should be taken into the pound.'

'And be put down if nobody claims her? That'd be a shame,' Beth said.

'Aye. But I suppose we'll be getting a fat bill for her keep one of these days.'

'As a matter of fact, you won't,' Beth said. We both

looked at her in surprise. 'An anonymous postal order, quite a large one, arrived with a typed note to say that it was for her keep, to save her from being destroyed. It was while you were still in hospital, John. Isobel and I decided that it was from some eccentric dog-lover.'

'Did you keep the envelope?'

'No. It was post-marked Glasgow, because we looked,' Beth said helpfully.

'I wonder,' the Sergeant said vaguely. 'Yon lassie . . . did she seem more interested in the dog, or in planting the description of the friend?'

'Damned if I know,' I said. 'Probably the dog.'

As the Sergeant left, I noticed dog-hairs on the back of his neat uniform. It was the season for coat-shedding. He might have brought them in with him, perhaps having collected them from a car-seat. I decided to go over the chairs with the small vacuum cleaner. The hairs would not show on our yellow-brown slip-covers but they would stand out on any dark clothing. They could have come off a dark yellow Labrador or a red setter, although they did not look quite right for either.

Five

Another week went by while I continued to mend. My left arm was still in a sling. It still hurt me if I tried to use it. I became adept at doing everything one-handed but dressing and undressing taxed my ingenuity and I usually let Beth help me. Besides being easier, it was more fun that way. In all other ways, I felt good.

The Sergeant visited us whenever he was passing but it seemed that the investigation was grinding slowly along without going anywhere, rather like the mills of God. Then, one morning, he telephoned me and from that moment things started to move again.

'Mr Cunningham?' he said. He had long since accepted that I dislike being credited with my former army rank.

'Speaking.'

'About the springer bitch, the one you call Anon. Somebody has made an offer to buy her.'

'From the executors?' I asked.

'There aren't any executors. As far as is known, he left no will; no relatives have turned up and such property as we've found comprises the ruined clothes on the body, one cartridge belt and a rusted wreck of a gun.'

'And a whistle,' I said.

'Yes. The receiver appointed to liquidate the remains of the business wants nothing to do with dogs. My superiors have decided that there's nothing more to be learned from her. So unless somebody takes her she'll be put down.'

The idea of a charming dog being destroyed because nobody cared was abhorrent to me. 'Accept the offer, then,' I said.

'I expect so,' he said. 'We can hold the money in case a claimant turns up. She'd have been handed over by now except that it seemed to me that it would only be right to give you a chance to offer for her.'

It took me only a few seconds to consider. 'If I could be absolutely positive of her identity,' I said, 'and if I could be sure that the pups she's carrying won't ruin her for life, I'd jump at it. She's an intelligent little animal and her breeding is first class. But no. If somebody wants her, let him have her and I hope he gives her a good life.'

'So be it,' he said.

It had been an easy decision to reach and yet it unsettled me for the day. Beth had often accused me of treating each purchaser of one of our pups as if he were asking for the hand of a favourite daughter. There was some truth in it. A dog is so vulnerable in the hands of a wrong or ignorant owner, capable of such an intense degree of misery, and so completely lacks any form of redress, that my imagination sometimes plays tricks on me. I never took Beth's comment to heart. She was as soft as I was.

That afternoon, the rain set in again. I persevered with training youngsters in the big barn but, when all the chores were done and the pups had been fed, we settled down in the big kitchen for tea, scones and a rambling discussion of business. Henry, who had walked over to join us, had swallowed his tea in what seemed to be a single gulp and was drinking my beer.

'I'm surprised that you didn't ask who was taking Anon,' Beth said suddenly out of the blue.

'I'd no right to the information,' I said. 'And on the whole I think I'd rather not know. I hope she's gone to a shooting man, but she'll probably be happy enough if she's become a house-pet.'

'You're just trying to convince yourself,' Isobel said tolerantly. There was no need to explain. Any working dog, prematurely retired, like many a man in the same position, pines for the old days of dedicated activity. It takes a lot of nothing, to fill time.

I dragged the conversation back to business and the eternal problem of choosing, long before there could be any signs of talent, which pups should be offered for sale as against which ones should be brought on for sale as trained dogs or for competition with an ultimate destiny as breeding stock. Isobel had the table covered with her file cards which we were passing around as if in a game of Happy Families when we heard tyres on the gravel. Nobody moved. With luck it would only be the postman.

The doorbell chimed. 'I'll go,' Beth said reluctantly, getting up. 'Don't decide anything until I come back.'

'I'll be surprised if we decide anything for a week,' Isobel said. We each had our own hunches and favourites.

Beth was back inside a minute. 'There's a man,' she said, holding out a card. 'I've put him in the sitting room. He wants to see all of us together but he won't say what it's about. He seems respectable,' she added uncertainly. We had been hoodwinked into admitting an itinerant bible-thumper not long before and he had been very difficult to dislodge.

I took the card and passed it to Isobel. According to his card, our visitor was a Mr E.J. Rodgers and he represented a well-known firm of Glasgow solicitors.

'We'd better see him,' Isobel said. 'Is the fire lit in your sitting room?' she asked Beth.

'Not yet. I could light it.'

'Don't bother. We're all tired – he can take us as

he finds us. Ask him if he'd mind stepping through here.'

'Should I leave the room?' Henry asked without moving.

'Not unless he wants you to,' Isobel said. 'Rest your ancient bones.'

E.J. Rodgers turned out to be a man of middle age, so perfectly turned out that he would almost have put Sergeant Ewell to shame. He belonged, I thought, under a glass bell. His black hair was parted along a geometrically perfect line. He was so freshly shaved that I was sure that he kept a battery razor in his car. The dark suit, white shirt and club tie had to be as nearly brand new as made no difference. Even his shoes seemed to have crossed our slightly muddy gravel in the rain without marring their perfect polish. Looking at him, one expected his features to be equally unblemished, but his face was slightly top-heavy. It was unbalanced by a bulbous nose and bore the scars of past acne.

Beth hung his dark coat and hat beside the boiler. I got up and turned one of the fireside chairs round, one-handed, so that he could face us. He thanked me and sat, careful not to stretch the perfect creases out of his trousers.

'You don't mind if we meet in the kitchen?' I said. 'It's cheerier in here.'

'And less formal,' he said. 'This is very suitable. A pleasant room. One feels at home.' His voice was deep with a faint trace of Glasgow in the vowels. He smiled briefly and got down to business. 'I asked to see you together because my errand is confidential and I'm advised that you three partners – plus Mr Kitts,' he added in Henry's direction, 'keep no secrets from each other. Also, I am to invite any one of the partners to undertake a . . . an errand on behalf of a client. I can speak in confidence? The matter is in no sense illegal,' he added quickly.

'On that understanding,' I said, 'we'll listen to you in confidence. That doesn't necessarily mean that we'll do whatever you ask.'

'That I accept, of course. Very well. On behalf of a client, I have obtained the springer spaniel bitch which was found in St Andrews and which you, Mrs Kitts, later identified as Salmon of Glevedale.'

'We called her Anon,' Beth said.

Mr Rodgers nodded politely. 'My client is at present in the United States,' he said, 'and wishes the . . . Anon to be delivered there. She could be sent by air as livestock, but there have been cases in which animals have been neglected in some warehouse.'

'There are firms which specialise in that sort of thing,' I said. 'They send a courier with the animal. Grooms with horses and that sort of thing.' My sentences sounded oddly truncated when compared with Mr Rodgers's rolling periods.

'My client is aware of that but is not confident that such a firm could be certain to produce somebody who was reliable, caring and discreet. And also, if it should prove necessary, enterprising enough to overcome any obstacles such as red tape.'

We considered the proposition in silence, exchanging glances rather than words. My first instinct was that one of us should accept. I could only too easily envisage the distress of a dog, separated from its late owner and despatched among strangers to some unknown fate. On the other hand, what seemed an extravagant way to transport a dog would make more sense as a trap – except that a trap would surely have been set for an individual, not for an unspecified member of a partnership.

Isobel's mind seemed to be working in the same

73

direction. 'Before we go any further,' she said, 'do you have any proof of your identity?'

For the first time, Mr Rodgers produced a full-blown smile. 'Very sensible,' he said. 'Perhaps you'll find something in here to satisfy you.' The question seemed to have been expected. From an inside pocket he produced a leather folder and handed it to Isobel. Its plastic envelopes held an assortment of credit and membership cards. With a gold fountain pen he signed his name on a slip of paper and passed it across. 'None of those cards bears my photograph,' he said, 'but you can compare signatures. If you still have any reservations, we can phone my office.'

Isobel returned the folder. 'You are E.J. Rodgers,' she said, 'WS, FCIArb and all the rest. We, on the other hand, are spaniel breeders and trainers. We're not in the transportation business.'

'But you do have a certain reputation for getting dogs to the right place at the right time and in the peak of condition,' Mr Rodgers said.

'You seem to know rather a lot about us,' I said. 'Have we been investigated? Or spied on?'

'Certainly not. One of my partners – Evan Lewis – judges at spaniel trials. I am authorised to offer a fee of a thousand US dollars over and above your travelling costs, for an errand which should take no more than three or four days at the most.'

A thousand dollars – about six hundred pounds at that time – represented a substantial part of the price of a trained dog and considerably more than our profit after our many outgoings – including the everlasting expenditure on dogfood – had been taken into account. 'Very generous,' I said. 'Over and above the cost of travelling to where exactly?'

'There, I must admit, is the rub,' Mr Rodgers said. 'My client's desire for confidentiality is such that the

"Need to Know" principle applies. Whoever acts as courier will only receive each instruction when it is required.'

'And those who remain here,' Isobel said, 'will know nothing.'

'That is so, at the time,' Mr Rodgers admitted. 'My client is perhaps being over-cautious but those are my instructions. I can only give you my personal assurance that my client does have a genuine regard for the dog and an equally genuine reason to keep the whole transaction as secret as possible.' He fell silent and waited for our comments. The message was clear. Take it or leave it. Make your mind up time.

Beth looked at me. 'I think you should do it,' she said.

I looked at her in mild surprise. She had been trying to tuck me up in bed ever since I left hospital and now she was encouraging me to go jauntering off to an unknown destination in the United States. 'I thought that you might go,' I said.

'Neither of us can spare the time,' Isobel said, 'and Henry isn't in the business. But you, you're still not ready for physical work although you're trying to help when you shouldn't. You won't need more luggage than you can put into a briefcase. A couple of days spent sitting around in aeroplanes and airport lounges might give you the physical rest you need but won't take.'

'And at the same time you could feel that you were doing something useful,' Beth said.

'Instead of getting in everybody's way? I don't fancy getting snowed up in Detroit or somewhere,' I said. According to the television, late blizzards were still sweeping across the Canadian border. I looked at Mr Rodgers. 'I'll do it if you'll give me one hint. Where I'd be going, would it be warm?'

'You certainly wouldn't encounter any snow,' he said cautiously, 'except perhaps to see it from aloft or through an airport window while in transit. Do you have a current passport?'

'Yes. No American visa, though.' I had been to the States, but not for some years.

'That can be taken care of. Give me your passport before I leave and it will meet you at the airport.'

'Which airport?' I asked.

'The one to which you will be taken by the car which will pick you up at eight a.m. tomorrow.' He saw my look of surprise. 'The sooner it's done, the less chance of a leak of information.'

That made sense, once you had accepted the need for extreme secrecy over the travel arrangements of a springer spaniel. 'We'll need one of those travelling boxes,' I said.

'That has already been obtained.'

'And you'd better leave Anon with us overnight. It'll be less unsettling for her if she gets used to me again. She'll need a certificate that her inoculations are up to date and another for her general health.

'I intended to have her taken to a vet this evening.'

'I am a vet,' Isobel said. 'We'll also want a letter of instructions on your firm's paper.'

Mr Rodgers smiled, almost laughing, and took an envelope from his pocket. 'If everybody was as sensible as you are, we solicitors would be out of business,' he said. 'You will be on your guard?'

'Very much so,' I said.

'And you will all— ?'

'None of us will discuss this except between ourselves,' Isobel said patiently.

'Then that would seem to be that.' Mr Rodgers, who had accepted a cup of tea, drank it without saying another word and left with my passport.

We made a fuss of Anon, who had been curled up on the back seat of Mr Rodgers's car under the eye of a chauffeur. I brought her back into the kitchen. She seemed genuinely pleased to see us. Some gundogs are like that. We had gone shooting together, so we were lifelong friends.

'But who on earth could his client be?' Beth asked plaintively. 'Not the man who tried to steal her?'

'Definitely not,' said Henry. He had been sitting so quietly that we had forgotten his presence. 'If we thought that, we'd have dissuaded John from the task. No, Mr Rodgers is who he says he is and represents a very respectable firm of solicitors. He might wander near the borderline of the law but he would never step across it.'

'Then who's the client?' Beth asked again. Anon, having greeted each of us, decided that Beth either had the most comfortable lap or would be the most tolerant host, and Beth allowed her to jump up and settle. 'Spoiled monkey!' Beth said.

'The widow, obviously,' Henry said. 'You'll note that Mr Rodgers never said "he" or "she", just "my client". We know that the dead man's wife visited him and we're told that she fell in love with the dog—'

'We were told that by the spurious Miss McGillivray,' I pointed out. 'And she wasn't what she seemed.'

'That doesn't necessarily mean that she was wrong on every count,' Henry said. 'Think about it. Who else but the widow might desperately want her late husband's dog but be quite determined not to let the dog lead the authorities to her?'

'Oh hell!' I said. 'This puts a new complexion on it. Oughtn't I to go to the police?'

'What with? You don't know any more than they do,' Henry said. 'They've already released Anon to Mr Rodgers. You only have my guess that she's his client. If you think about the sequence of events, you'll see that it's very unlikely that she ever saw any money from the

British swindle, while the proceeds from the Savings and Loan fraud are American business. Do the errand and you may be free to tell the police something useful.'

'And besides,' Beth said, 'you promised.' In her view, that was the clinching argument.

Anon slept on our feet that night. This was in flat contradiction of our rules and principles, because we could hardly admit one dog to the house without admitting them all. (Jason was an occasional exception.) But we were in no mood for another midnight escapade.

When the car arrived, on time, in the morning and Beth saw us both off, I thought that she put more emotion into her farewell to the dog. Which, I supposed, was only fair – she was saying goodbye forever to Anon, while I expected to be back within a few days.

The car was a hired Rover, its driver skilled but uncommunicative. We joined the motorway but came off again two interchanges later, at Kinross. Not Turnhouse, then.

Anon, sprawling across my lap, seemed unperturbed. Most dogs would have shown anxiety but, bearing in mind her time adrift in St Andrews, she had remarkable confidence in her own future and in the essential benevolence of mankind. It was evident that she had been well treated – even by her last owner, a man who had not jibbed at robbing the small saver. Perhaps, like many another, he had cared more for dogs than for his fellow men. I was in no position to be critical. I was just as capable of the anthropomorphism of dogs, and of giving affection where I knew that it would be returned. It did not of itself make me a bad person or a good one.

We crossed Kincardine Bridge and the car was filtered effortlessly through the late rush-hour traffic of Glasgow. We passed the turn-off for Renfrew. Not a shuttle to London, but Prestwick.

A young man from Mr Rodgers's office was waiting with the white plastic travelling box and my passport. He took over my luggage – one briefcase with a book, razor, toothbrush, pyjamas and a polythene bag of biscuit meal – and stayed with me. We had time to give Anon a walk on the grass and then she was settled in the box and I was in the queue to check in for the plane to Boston. The new security precautions were being taken very seriously but the contents of my briefcase were obviously innocent. They wanted to X-ray Anon in case she had been induced to swallow a bomb but when I explained that she was pregnant they excused her. I could only glimpse her through the ventilation holes but I thought that she gave me one anxious look as the baggage conveyor took her away.

The young man escorted me to the boarding gate before giving me my tickets and boarding pass. I glanced through the tickets. Boston – Memphis – Houston. Each ticket was in a different name.

The in-flight movie was rubbish. I dozed and read to Boston. The airline seemed to feed us whenever it was a mealtime by local time. Flying with the sun, mealtimes did not come around very often. I thought about Beth. At the last moment she had added a pair of clean underpants to my bag. 'You may get caught up in a bomb scare,' she said. It came to me suddenly what she had meant. I shook with private laughter but nobody paid any attention. They probably thought that I was watching the film.

If ever I take to smuggling as a profession, I shall take a dog along with me. From the moment when Anon came off the luggage carousel in Boston, everybody from baggage handlers to the immigration officials were more interested in her than they were in me. Where was she going? Was she trained to the gun? Was she thirsty? Any one of them would cheerfully have dropped everything and gone to fetch water. Somebody had even cleaned out the tray in the bottom of the box.

I could have checked her through to Houston but I thought that she might be comforted by the sound of a familiar voice during the wait at Memphis. We shared a hamburger there and I collected her for the last time at Houston-Hobby airport. She was beginning to fret, but only about her dinner which was long overdue. It was around eleven p.m. in Houston but almost dawn at home. I opened my polythene bag of kennel meal and fed and watered her while I wondered what happened next.

Another young man appeared – even younger than the one at Prestwick. He had the sort of face which used to be typecast as the boy next door. He sported a crew cut, sneakers, jeans, a T-shirt and a baseball cap. I had noticed him earlier, circulating in the background and watching faces. 'Captain Cunningham?' he asked, with an accent on the last syllable.

'Just Mister,' I said. 'Mr Cunningham.'

We shook hands. I was still wearing my sling, as much to warn others not to bump into my shoulder as for any real need, but he picked up Anon in her travelling box and firmly removed my briefcase from my grasp. 'Come this way, sir,' he said.

'Happily,' I said. 'I've had enough flying for the moment.'

'You're not finished yet, sir.'

He led me off the beaten track and through a parking garage on to the street. We stepped over low fences. It became soft underfoot and by the lights of traffic – so close that I could feel the wind of its passing – I saw that we were on grass. The young man waited politely while I let Anon out of her box. She hurried a few polite paces from us, squatted down and then came to heel. We walked on together, hopping more low fences, towards some buildings with a sign that read AVITAT. Toylike aircraft, looking ridiculously small after the monsters in which I had spent almost a day and a night, were lined up outside.

At a desk inside, a man was drinking coffee and watching a small television set. 'You found him, then?' he said, without taking his eyes off the screen.

'Yep. How much do I owe you?'

The man chuckled at something on the TV. 'Hell, you ain't been here long enough to charge you parking,' he said absently. 'Ain't no one else coming in tonight. Gimme thirty-three fifty for the gas and oil and remember to use us again next time you come to town, hear?'

'I'll sure as hell do that,' the boy said. He turned to me. 'It's the Cessna one-fifty out there, sir. I'll be a minute. You better have a pee, it's a long way and no pit stops.'

With some difficulty, one-handed, I lifted Anon up into the small two-seater plane, settled her in my lap and passed the strap around both of us. The boy arrived almost on our heels and stowed my briefcase and the box behind the seats. He began an exchange with the tower. I fell into a doze. It had been a long day. I was vaguely aware of the plane taxiing around the endless taxiways at Hobby and the increase of noise as we took off.

About two hours later I felt a change of motion and snapped awake. Anon, on my knee, was sitting up and taking an intelligent interest in the instruments and the night outside. By now, she considered herself to be a seasoned flyer.

A small cluster of lights was showing to port. The boy saw me looking. 'Jersey Lily,' he said loudly over the engine's noise.

'Who?'

'Langtry, Texas. That's Mexico beyond.' He set a new course on his compass.

We flew on. I think that I dozed again. I felt the plane slow and begin a descent. On the ground a light showed and, nearer, a glow which I thought would be from the headlamps of a car facing away from us. As we came lower, I could make out the car's tail lamps. He brought the lights into line, switched on his landing lights at the last moment and set the plane down gently. When we had rolled almost to a halt he turned and taxied back to the car. 'We're here, sir,' he said.

'Where's here?'

'This is. It's an old dirt strip made by the dope smugglers.'

The engine cut and died. He climbed out stiffly. I heard a woman's voice. Anon pricked up her ears and then did a flying leap through the open door. I followed more slowly, stepping down on to a surface of dirt and occasional weeds. The air was warm, warmer than most summer days in Scotland.

The woman's figure was vague against the dazzle of the car's headlights, but I saw that Anon was up in her arms and the woman was having to twist her neck to avoid getting a well-licked face. 'You remember Mommy?' she said delightedly. 'Or is it the cookies you remember, my darling?' She put the spaniel down and nodded to me. 'Hi!'

'Hello!' I said.

She switched her attention to the young pilot. 'Jim, could you be back here at eight, to take Captain Cunningham back to Houston?'

'Yessum,' he said. 'No problem. You'll remember . . . ?'

'I'll remember. You can have the car, free and clear, if I'm sure you haven't run off at the mouth.'

'No fear of that, ma'am.' He bent to look at his

watch in the light of the car's lamps. 'I'll be going. Still time for three to four hours' sleep. Be seeing you, sir.'

He turned away and climbed into the plane. Two minutes later he was a diminishing murmur in what I thought was the east. I felt alone and vulnerable. If the lady was so concerned to cover her tracks, I could be the only inconvenient witness. But no hard men emerged from the darkness and I told myself not to be a fool. I could have been more easily knocked off at home, and far more cheaply.

She deposited Anon gently in the back of the car, sat into the left-hand seat and leaned across to push the other door open. Until my tired brain remembered about left-hand drives I thought that she was inviting me to take the wheel. She left her door open so that the courtesy light remained on. I saw that she was in her thirties with brown hair so bleached by the sun as to be almost blonde. She was attractive but, although her other features were feminine, a square jaw gave her face a determined and almost manly look. Her silk blouse contrasted with her denim jacket and skirt.

'Captain— '

'Just Mister,' I said.

'Mr Cunningham, I'm grateful. You've brought her here, safe and sound.'

'And pregnant,' I said. 'You knew that?'

'They told me. No matter. The more the merrier.' From a tooled leather shoulder-bag on the seat beside her, she produced a booklet of traveller's cheques and began scribbling an illegible signature on each of them. 'Ten cheques, each for a hundred bucks. Right?'

'That's right,' I said.

'Did you have any expenses?'

I decided to let her away with the cost of the hamburger. 'Not a thing.'

'If you have to pay out anything on your way home, get in touch with Mr Rodgers.'

She closed the door, cutting off the light and my view of a figure which was all feminine and very piquant. The cheques were pressed into my hand and the car moved off, apparently of its own accord.

The vehicle was a large estate car. It absorbed the bumps in the uneven airstrip as though running on tarmac. The light in the runway turned out to be an electric lantern. She opened her door and scooped it up without stopping, handing it to me to switch off and dump behind the seats while she U-turned. 'Where the hell . . . ?' she muttered to herself. Then a gap showed up in the scrub beside the runway and she turned on to a track which had seen little use for years.

The car made light of the rough and undulating surface. I could not identify the model but it seemed almost new and remarkably well appointed. With the seat down, the rear would have held a dozen dog-cages. It was cool inside and I realised that it was air-conditioned. It was, in fact, exactly what I needed to replace my smaller and worn-out vehicle.

I felt a pang of envy. 'You're giving this car to that boy?' I asked curiously. 'Giving it?'

'Why not?' she said. 'I'll have finished with it in a few days. He wants it more than money. His daddy won't give him a car.'

'Just an aeroplane?'

'Right. His daddy thinks cars are dangerous. And he's damn right. There's more room in the sky. But,' she said, nursing the car over a steep hump, 'a gift from an old family friend would be hard to refuse. Have you figured out yet who I am?'

'My guess is that you're the widow of Mr Peregrine Hawker Falconer.'

By the light from the instruments I saw her nod.

'I thought you'd guess Falconer,' she said. 'Hawker maybe. I never thought you'd know about Peregrine. I knew somebody'd made the connection but I didn't know that anybody outside the cops had it yet. You found his body, didn't you? So my lawyer said.'

'Yes. My wife saw it . . . him first.'

'They're . . . sure that it was him?' It was half statement and half question.

'They've found the car he hired,' I said carefully. 'The fingerprints inside it matched those sent over by the FBI along with an Identikit. The landlady at the Stoneleigh Hotel recognised the Identikit. It seems to connect up.'

'I was sure of it,' she said, almost under her breath, 'but I kept wondering if Dave wasn't pulling another flimflam.'

The track brought us to a main road. It was empty, no lights showing for a mile in either direction, but she sat there, silent. I wondered whether she was coming belatedly to terms with her widowhood.

'I guess we're not being followed just now,' she said suddenly. She pulled across the road and turned left.

'I certainly didn't bring any followers,' I said.

She produced a mellow laugh. Widowhood was not sitting too heavily on her. 'If you had, Jim would have taken you somewhere quite different and left you stranded. No, you've played it straight and I'm grateful. But there was somebody trying to stick to my tail earlier, only he couldn't make it in an old pick-up. A Bubba,' she added.

'Who?'

'Don't you have them where you come from? I thought I'd seen one at least. There's no mistaking a Bubba. Given names William Robert, for sure; Billybob for short. Or, as often, he's known as Bubba. They say it's short for Brother but others say it comes from the way we Texans talk with our mouths full. Some places, the men call each other Bubba the way in New York they call each other Jack.'

'Or Jimmy in Glasgow,' I said.

'Is that right? He wears a beard and one of those gimme caps from a tractor company. A vest – what you call a waistcoat – over a workshirt. Jeans with a belly bulging above the belt. He used to wear cowboy boots but now he wears sneakers. And he thinks he's as tough as hell. Mostly they're good guys, they just look mean, but there's some bad bastards among them.'

'We have them,' I said. 'Not exactly the same, but near enough. Why would he be following you?'

'God knows. That's what worries me. You can hire a Bubba for almost anything, especially if you tell him a good tale. But not the Feds, they don't work that way. My fear is that somebody thinks I'm holding the money Dave grabbed in California. And I'm not, thank God!' She drove in silence for a mile or two. 'I'd take us to a motel if there was a motel within easy driving. As it is, I could pull over and let you get some sleep in the back. You must be dead beat and your poor arm and all.' The car slowed.

'I've woken up again now,' I said. 'I'm more hungry than anything else. But I can survive. If you'd rather drive around or wait it out until Jim comes back, that's all right. Or drop me back at the airstrip. It's warm enough for sleeping out.'

The car picked up again to the legal fifty-five, through countryside which seemed to comprise miles and miles of damn-all. 'I should have thought about that. I'd forgotten how the airlines feed you on small scraps of plastic these days. And you've been on the move since about this time yesterday. I'm getting kind of starved myself, just thinking about it. I guess there's no harm taking you back to the old homestead. There's still some food in the freezer. Only one bed made up, though, but that needn't worry you if you don't want it to.'

The last few words were said in the tone in which one might invite a neighbour in for coffee but the implication was clear. 'For all that's left of the night,' I said, 'an armchair would do.'

'Kind of slow to take a hint, aren't you?' she said. 'You've been straight with me and I still feel that I owe you. If you're worried by your arm, there's ways. Surely you're not gay?'

I could hardly say that the threat of infection had rather taken the shine off infidelity, nor would male pride let me admit that exhaustion and illness had put any kind of sexual performance out of the question. 'I've only been married for a few months,' I said.

'Your first marriage?' she said.

'Yes.'

'I think that's cute,' she said after a moment's thought. There was a smile in her voice. 'Real nice. Forget that I spoke.'

'I won't forget,' I said. 'I take it as a great compliment.'

'You're sweet,' she said. 'And I just love your accent.'

'I don't have an accent,' I said. It seemed an easy way to turn the subject. But she let the talk die as she turned off the main road and followed a dirt road in the general direction of Mexico. After about two miles we came over a slight rise to see a ranch house in front of us. The place was well kept but the barns looked empty. There was a total absence of life – no horses beyond the neat rails, no sound of cattle, not even a farm cat.

'This is it,' she said. 'I was born and raised here and it's my home for another day or two. After that, goodbye forever. Come along inside.'

We got out of the car. She slung her bag over her shoulder and lifted Anon out of the back. As she straightened up with the spaniel bitch in her arms, lights blazed suddenly from a vehicle parked deep in one of the barns.

Six

'Put the dog down, lady, and stand back,' said a voice. I had thought that her accent was strong, but the new voice had an accent which could have chopped logs.

I had just put my hand into my pocket for a handkerchief. I left it there. Better not to move again. He would know that I had not grabbed for a pistol. My companion stood uncomfortably poised, with Anon clutched to her chest and her large bag looped over her shoulder. 'What the hell?' she said.

A figure moved forward into the light, only ten yards from us. 'Bubba!' she said under her breath. The figure was in silhouette but what I could see answered her description, beard, belly and all. It also held a pump-action shotgun as though it was accustomed to using it.

'Just do as I say, lady,' the man said. 'It's only the dog I'm being paid for and I don't lightly work for free, but it'd be as easy to kill all three of you.' He might mean it or he might not, but the only thought in my mind was that an armed criminal who has shot once will shoot again . . .

Anon was wriggling to get down and explore this new environment but my companion held on tight. 'But why?' she asked shrilly.

'Lady, I don't know why and I don't care. Just do as I tell you or I'll blast the mutt whether you're holding it or not. And then I'll have to go on shooting until there's nobody alive around here but me.' His voice was louder, as though he was taking pleasure from a sense of power.

The fumes of tiredness had blown away and my old training had taken over. My mind was furiously calculating the odds. Even if, as seemed unlikely, this man – Bubba – would draw the line when he had killed the dog, Anon was my friend. I had been taught to take action. When the odds are hopeless, any act, however desperate, is better than to leave the initiative in the other man's hands. From where I stood I would just have a chance of surviving a dive which would sweep the three of us behind the car. It was a slim chance of escaping unshot into the most temporary of havens, and what it would do to my injured shoulder I preferred not to think, but my earlier training had programmed me against inaction but without suggesting anything better than this desperate resort.

I braced myself for sudden movement, slid my left arm out of the sling and jerked my other hand, flicking the coins from my pocket against the nearest wall. The noise from outside his area of attention disturbed the man and he swung away. But at the same moment my companion sighed and stooped to place Anon on the ground. She gave the spaniel a pat, as though in farewell, and stood erect again.

As I made my dive, she moved with equal suddenness, almost spoiling my move. A shot sounded, a double slam. The first part of the sound was thin and sharp for a shotgun. My mind was racing and I had time to think, crazily, that his gun had double-discharged. My shoulder caught the lady at the waist and we slid together over the bonnet of the car, a tangle of legs and arms. We landed together, heavily. I had lost my chance of grabbing Anon but below the car I could see that, true to her training, she had sat down at the sound of the shot, a waiting target. She seemed unhurt, but gunshot victims are sometimes unaware of having been hit.

Then the pain took over. I had landed on my wounded shoulder and something terrible was happening deep inside me. I was just aware that my companion was disentangling herself and getting up. I tried to grab and pull her down but I was lying on my good arm. I waited for another shot to finish her but all was silent except for the ringing in my ears.

'Are you hit?' asked a voice. A female voice. It seemed to be aimed at me. We must both be alive, more or less, for the moment.

'Don't think so,' I mumbled. I managed to drag my eyes open. Anon was still sitting, waiting for the order to retrieve.

Then I saw, between the front wheels, that the man had crumpled. He was down on the ground. There was a long scar through the dirt between us. He made some noises, twitched for a few seconds, gave the sigh of a man who has been afraid but has released his breath because he is afraid no more. I sat up, very carefully. My companion walked forward, a blued revolver held in readiness, and bent over him.

As the pain relaxed its grip on me little by little, it was replaced by a greater unease of the mind. Nothing made sense. As far as I could see, we were still alone.

'What happened?' I asked her. My voice sounded as if it came from a long way off.

'I shot him,' she said matter-of-factly but in a thin, high voice. 'Clean through the heart, I think. Well, no point having a gun unless you learn to shoot it.' She holstered the revolver through an opening in the end of her shoulder-bag. She patted the bag. 'Smith and Wesson's new LadySmith thirty-eight in the Feminine Protection holster-purse.' She came back and stood over me. 'That was brave. Brave and gallant but stupid. If you'd been quicker by just one instant, you'd've spoiled my shot and we'd both be dead. But I guess you couldn't know what I was up to any more than I could guess what you were going to do. Maybe I was stupid, too. I just don't know.' She rubbed her elbows. 'You nearly flattened me. How you doing? What happened to your face and your arm anyway?'

'Somebody tried to steal your dog once before,' I said. My voice now came out as a husky croak. 'I got stabbed. Just now, I came down on it.'

'She seems to be unlucky for you. We'd best take a look at it. Come along inside. Can you walk?' There was a slight tremor in her voice now that the shock was catching up with her.

'Help me up,' I said. 'I'm no great weight.'

She looked hard into the shadows and then took my hand. She was strong. She pulled me effortlessly to my feet and led us into the house and through a hallway into a spacious kitchen. The room was large and plain but the equipment seemed to me to be the latest.

I had lived through enough action during my army days not to be shocked by death itself, but my life since then had conditioned me to believe that civilians do not shoot civilians without endless repercussions. What little I knew about justice in the southern USA, culled mostly from books and films, inspired little confidence, while Bubba himself must have had friends. I pulled out a chair from the central table and collapsed shakily into it. Anon curled up beside the stove, quite at home.

My companion had disappeared. She returned in a few minutes and again holstered her pistol. 'If there's anybody else out there, I don't know where the hell he is,' she said. 'Let's take a look at you.'

Very gently but with fingers which trembled slightly, she opened my jacket and shirt. 'You're just skin and bone,' she said. 'There's nothing showing except a scar about a month old. You need a doctor?'

'I think I've torn the muscle apart again,' I said. The pain was still abating, very slowly, as long as I kept my shoulder still. I could tolerate it. 'Nothing to do but rest it. Listen, we must call the sheriff or somebody.'

'Shut up while I think. Do you drink coffee? I suppose you'd rather have tea.'

'Coffee, please,' I said. I had tasted American tea on my previous visits.

'I need a minute.' She stood and breathed deeply a dozen times and then swung into action. The process of thought did not seem to interfere with her ability as a cook. She darted between the worktop, a large fridge and the microwave oven. A mug of fragrant coffee appeared in front of me with a jug of cream and a bowl of sugar.

'Steak, ham and eggs,' she said. 'Grits or French fries?'

I chose French fries. Whatever grits might be, they did not sound appetising. With my first sip of the coffee I felt ready to dribble down my chin. I was surprised that I could feel hunger while my thoughts were in turmoil. I had done nothing and yet I felt as guilty as if I had killed Bubba myself. Deeply entrenched feelings about good and evil, the sanctity of life and the power of the law boiled to the surface of my mind. But I was off my home territory. First, wait to discover what her thoughts produced.

She cut my steak up for me and we ate in silence. When we had finished, she pushed her plate away and lit a cigarette.

'Here's the way it is,' she said. She was as calm as she had been in the car. 'That bastard was going to kill us for sure, you know that?'

'I couldn't swear to it,' I said.

'You won't have to. Just remember that he wasn't

paying a social visit. He may've been after the dog, though why the hell anyone should want to knock off my baby I'm damned if I know. But he sure as hell wouldn't leave us around to talk about it.'

'So why did he tell you to put the dog down?' I asked.

'Think about it. You're the man, he'd expect you to be the more dangerous. If he hit you first, I might have let the dog run and jumped the other way. But if we believed him and waited while he killed Salmon, he could take you next and then me. Anyway, that's how I had it figured in the heat of the moment. Not that it makes any difference. Around here, if some Bubba or a Mex points a gun at you, you try like hell to get your shot off first.

'Here's what we'll do. We'll leave here at first light and I'll drop you off at the airstrip. You'll have a wait for Jim, but that can't be helped. I'll drive straight from there to the sheriff's office.' She made a face. 'It's a darned shame. I was going to fade away in the next day or two. I've already sold the place to Jim's dad – he bought most of the land some years back and now he wants the house for Jim's sister who's marrying in the fall.'

'You might be better to skip out now,' I said.

She shook her head. 'The last thing I want is a hue and cry. That way, if they ever caught up with me, flight would be evidence of guilt. I'll have to stay and see it through and hope like hell that nobody makes the connection between me and the late Dave until after I'm gone.'

'They'll charge you,' I said. 'Manslaughter at the least.'

She looked amazed that I should even think such a thing. 'No chance. Not if you get the hell out of here and keep your mouth shut. See how I trust you? Can you give me a week to ride it out?'

It was all wrong and yet . . . 'I promise. But will a week be enough?'

'I knew you were a right guy. A week'll be plenty. We're west of the Pecos now. Times have moved on, but the law is still on the rough and ready side. Look at it this way. My family has lived around here forever. We've been good neighbours and helped to build this country. Our name's worth something hereabouts. I went to school with the sheriff. I'm a woman living alone while my husband's away on business. I came home to find this Bubba threatening me with a gun. It'll turn out that he had a bad reputation, or why would he have taken on a job like this? I can bet you that this ol' boy has been around town, showing his ass and acting smart and there's already been word to the sheriff that this sucker was in town.

'He said that he wanted money but he had rape in his mind. So I shot him. Any other girl would have done the same. He'd pulled down the phone-wires – I'll do that before we leave. So I stayed in the house until daylight, just in case he had some friends with him. It'll hardly make the papers, even.'

If she was confident, it was not for me to make objections. I wanted nothing more than a quick exit from the scene. 'What will you do afterwards?' I asked her.

She poured us some more coffee while she thought about it. 'I don't think I'll tell you too much about that,' she said at last. 'I trust you, but I want a complete break and nobody in the know. I'll just tell you this much. I have an old friend. He wanted me to marry him, before even I met Dave. I guess now's his chance. We used to hunt together. That's how I came to meet Dave, we all came together on a trip to shoot quail. So I guess Salmon here won't be short of a job.' She lit another cigarette and blew smoke at the ceiling. 'Why in hell is somebody so interested in this one dog. Does she know where the treasure's buried or something?'

'We've wondered the same.'

'I'll keep her near me and a gun near my fist until I can make my move,' she said.

My part in these plans seemed to be very much that of a rat leaving a sinking ship. On the other hand, I could see that my presence might provoke questions which she would very much prefer not to be asked.

'Say, I could use a shower,' she said, 'but I can't go to the sheriff smelling sweet and fresh. Wrong image for a woman who's been sweating all night. How about you? No reason why you shouldn't take a shower.'

If I took my clothes off I would never be able to don them again unaided; and the thought of being nursemaided by this tough, competent Amazon terrified me. I decided that I should gather some information while we were in this state of trust. Besides, I was curious. 'I don't even know your real name,' I said.

She shrugged. 'You could find it out easy enough if you tried. So why not? I'm Jessica Wendell Holbright. Born Wendell, married Holbright. You can call me Jess – most people do. I guess that was what put all those falconry names into Dave's mind – jesses, hawks, you know?'

'I know,' I said. A jess is the strap on a falcon's leg.

'Dave always did go for the great outdoors. Camping, hunting . . . And he saw himself as a hawk and all the others as doves. He certainly made a grab at me.'

'Tell me about him.'

She looked at me thoughtfully. 'Can't do any harm, I guess,' she said at last.

'I had some money, you see, after my folks died. Not a whole lot, by Texan standards, but some. When Dave and I married, he thought that he'd get his hooks into my little pile, but no way! And I wouldn't sell the place either. I made him a good allowance.' I saw her breasts rise and fall in a sigh. 'Well, maybe that was a mistake, it hurt his pride. He wanted to be the breadwinner and the man of property – and he always had this streak of ruthlessness. He pulled one or two shady deals and then took off for California, telling me that he was on to a good thing.'

She sighed again, more deeply. 'And he could have been. He was a clever man but stupid, you know what I mean?'

'A clever fool?' I said. 'I know what you mean. Universities are full of them.'

'Yeah. Well, Dave went and set up this Savings and Loan thing and lit out with the money. He'd have been better to stay with it and remain legit, because there's no bigger fool than a con artist when he gets out of his league and he got taken for a ride in a deal over some Mex gold and lost the lot. And meanwhile one of the parcels of land which he'd bought cheap, as window dressing for the Savings and Loan, turned out to be the one place for a new freight terminal. Wouldn't you know it? The receiver who'd been put in was a bright young whizz-kid. He sold it for a packet and parlayed the money up until he could pay off all the investors. Most of them left the money to ride, I hear. So I guess they haven't been looking for him too hard over this side.

'While this was happening, Dave had skipped out of the country to let the dust settle and was set to recoup his losses by another con over your side of the water. That's why I went over, to try and convince him that he wasn't at the top of the hit-list over here and that nobody knew him from a rat's ass anyway. I said that I'd split my roll with him if he'd only come home, for God's sake, and settle down. But he was in too deep, by then. He promised me . . . But what the hell?

Promises come cheap and somebody killed him before he could make good.' She looked past my shoulder into the distance, blinking. 'He was a louse, but he was good to me when he thought about it,' she finished.

'Tell me about your visit to Scotland,' I said.

She looked at me with her head on one side and then decided that a little more revelation could not matter. I think that she was glad to talk, to keep her mind off what might have been. 'I flew to Gatwick,' she said, 'and he met me off the shuttle at Edinburgh.' She pronounced Edinburgh exactly as it is spelled. 'We spent the most of a week wrangling about when he'd come back. But there were good times too. I'll have them to remember. He took me to shoot your red grouse once. It cost an arm and a leg but it was worth it.' She pulled a wry face. 'I paid for it out of my own bankroll, so you needn't think I was living it up on hot money. The moor was real pretty, the heather almost scarlet and all, and those grouse come like bullets. I never saw birds fly like that.

'And Salmon was great, weren't you, my darling?' Anon gave a little whimper of acknowledgment. 'They let me walk with the beaters as a flank gun in the afternoon and she worked her little ass off in that long heather.'

'He had a shooting friend,' I said. 'Somebody who hasn't come forward, so it's a reasonable guess that he was your husband's associate in the fraud. And the money hasn't shown up, so another guess, unless you know better, would be that that's who killed your husband and why.'

'I hadn't thought about it that way,' she said, 'but I suppose it's so. Will they get the bastard? Dave wasn't much, but far's I know he drew the line at murder.'

'From what I hear, they're stuck at the moment. It seems that both men were cagey about their association. You never met the other man?'

98

'Never. And Dave was as close as an oyster about him. Cagey, like you said. From what little he did say, they went after geese a few times in the early mornings and Dave would go back for breakfast and to get warmed up at the other man's place, but I don't know where that was. Dave did say once what a help the other man had been.'

'You're sure?' I asked quickly. 'You're sure that he was saying that his shooting companion had also helped him in the big fraud? They couldn't have been two different men?'

'That's how it came over to me. It seemed to me that Dave had sought out this cookie as being just the guy he needed. Something he said made me think he knew the guy's name before ever he went across.'

'He'd need an introduction to somebody,' I said. 'He couldn't just turn up in Scotland and start asking people, "How would you like to help me with a fraud?" Somebody must have given him either the right name or the name of somebody else who could fix him up with the right introduction.'

'I bet you're right. Then, I guess, when they found that they were both sold on hunting, they got together now and again, but being very careful not to be seen around together. I think I set eyes on him once, though.'

She said the last few words so casually that it took me some seconds to recognise what might be the Open Sesame for which the police had been waiting. 'Could you describe him?' I asked.

'It was only a glimpse. And I couldn't appear as a witness,' she said, 'or some shitass would want to haul me up as an accessory or something. But if there's a chance that he killed Dave or set him up, I'll tell you what I know.

'It was the evening before we went to the moor together. Dave didn't have a spare gun for me and I like

99

a faster-handling gun than a twelve-gauge. He said that his pal had a sixteen-gauge or else that he knew where to borrow one for me, I forget. He made a phone-call and a little later he went downstairs to meet his buddy and get the gun.'

'How much later?' I asked.

'Maybe an hour, I wasn't watching the clock. If you're hoping to make a guess at the distance,' she said shrewdly, 'he maybe didn't set off straight away. I was upstairs, looking out what I was going to wear next day. I didn't want some bum thinking that Texans can't dress right. I looked out of our bedroom window – not being curious, you understand, but just wanting to be sure that Dave was getting me a gun, because I didn't want to miss the chance of trying my hand at red grouse. They were just getting the gun and some shells out of the trunk of his car.

'I was looking down from above, so I never saw his face. The impression I got was that he had a round head. And he was very deep-chested. It was like looking down on a beach ball on top of a barrel. He had dark brown hair, parted on the left, no bald spot. And sticking-out ears. That's all I saw.'

It might not be much but it might eliminate a hundred suspects. 'What about his car?' I asked.

'Just one of your compacts. Not big or small. Colour ... grey, I think. It was a saloon with a trunk, not a station wagon. Hell, I didn't give it more than a glance.'

'The gun, then,' I said. She was a woman but she was Texan. She would know about shotguns. 'You must have given that more than a glance. You had it in your hands for most of a day.'

I was right, she did know about guns. Most British women, even Beth, would have become vague; but Americans take the gun seriously. 'It shot like a dream,' she said. 'I wanted Dave to try and buy it for me before I came back, but he said no dice. A side-by-side bored skeet and improved. Sidelock. Short barrels, twenty-five inch I'd guess. Not new but a good gun, an Italian copy of a Best English. I was getting better than three for five shots, which I'm told is good.' She stopped and laughed to herself. 'Some of the menfolk were looking at me kind of glassy-eyed, as if a woman was only there on sufferance and I'd no business being able to shoot better than some of them, but there was one of your lords there, Crail was his name, he was running the show, he was real friendly – not the way you think a lord would be – and he said that if I'd been over for longer he'd've given me an invite to see what I could do with driven pheasants.'

What she had told me could be a help to the police but, although sixteen-bores are out of fashion in Britain, there were plenty of guns around which answered that description, superficially at least. I could not see the police solemnly measuring the choke boring of bankers' guns. I asked whether there had been anything distinctive about the engraving, but it had been the usual rose and scroll.

'You told me that he brought cartridges,' I said. 'Was there a gunshop name on the box?'

She shook her head emphatically. 'Gamebore and Eley, mixed up in a cartridge bag. All sevens,' she said.

I racked my brain but tiredness had caught up with me again as the adrenalin wore off. I was trying to think through a quilt of exhaustion. 'All this could help the police,' I said. 'Not to find him, but to identify him once he's been found. Do you mind if I pass it on, after a few days?'

Her face had softened while she spoke about the good times but now her jaw looked firm again. 'Go right ahead. I'd like to think that I'd helped finger the bastard for what he did to Dave and maybe stopped him doing it to somebody else. Let me know through Mr Rodgers if they get him – I'll send him a Glad You're In There card once a year. And now, we'll have to get ready to move. Time for one more cup of coffee to see you on the road.'

We had one last cup of coffee and then she washed up carefully. 'What about the dog?' I said. 'Won't that suggest another visitor?'

'I've been talking for weeks about the cute little spaniel Dave bought in Scotland. So he shipped her over and Jim fetched her from Houston. Big deal!'

Jess took a careful look around to ensure that I had left no traces of my presence. Then we went outside. In the first light of dawn the body was lying on its back, the shotgun beside one outflung arm, the very picture of an aggressor cut down in the act. The lights of the pick-up had dimmed to a red glow in the barn.

Anon went on to the back seat of the car. Jess was about to drive off when I called, almost shouted, to stop.

'Now what?' she said.

'I threw some coins against the wall to distract Bubba's attention.'

'You worried about the money?'

'British coins,' I said. 'They might make even the most friendly sheriff think.'

She slapped her forehead. 'You're right.'

The tenderness in my shoulder seemed to have invaded my whole body. Jess got out of the car and gathered the coins. She drove halfway to the road and then stopped to use a tow-rope from the car to pull down the telephone wires, refusing my half-hearted offer of help. We set off again. The sun topped the horizon. The country looked dead and burnt but she

102

said that it would be green in a few more weeks. After
that she drove in silence until we had turned off on to
the track which led to the airstrip.

'I'll send you a message,' she said suddenly. 'It'll be
– oh – "Spring has come at last". When you get those
words, you'll know that I'm free and clear and you can
tell the cops all you know. Until then . . . '

'Until then, I won't say a word.'

'You promise?'

'I promise.'

She pulled up on the edge of the airstrip. 'You're
a good scout,' she said. 'Your wife's a lucky girl.' She
turned in her seat and kissed me warmly on the lips. It
went on and on. There was no passion in it. I could
not have told why the experience was pleasant, but I
shall remember that kiss when I am very old. I was in
no hurry to break away.

'I must go and act the terrified little woman,' she
said at last. 'Jim will be here before too long. Tell him
from me that he brought Salmon to me from Houston,
the day before yesterday. Now go.'

I twisted round, despite my shoulder, and gave Anon
a scratch behind the ear. I knew that I would never see
her again and I had developed an affection for the little
bitch. Then I collected my bag and got out of the car.
Jess drove in a circle and waved once before dragging a
trail of dust along the track. I sat on a rock and watched
a small herd of antelope graze across the burnt-out
landscape in the middle distance. There was heat in the
sun, but before it could get uncomfortable there came
a droning in the sky and Jim arrived, early, setting the
plane down as gently as if it had been crystal and taxiing
to within a few yards of me.

He flew me to Houston and I went home by
Detroit, Boston and back to Prestwick through another
night. I slept, on and off, for much of the way, but in

my waking moments I thought about Jess Holbright, wondering whether the sheriff had accepted her story. If not, her easiest escape might be to put the blame on me. Only when the long-haul jumbo had dragged itself into the air from Boston airport did I realise that I had been sitting with my fists clenched, half expecting men in dark suits and raincoats to arrive and take me off the plane.

Jess would have had the busiest day of her life and yet she had not forgotten about me. She must have made a surreptitious phone-call. The same car was waiting at Prestwick to take me home.

Seven

After the brown of Texas the green of Scotland was
blinding. The shrubs in the garden must have been
in bloom when I left but I had not noticed them
until homecoming blessed me with fresh vision. Beth,
beautiful Beth, still looking ten years less than her real
age, came flying out to greet me. I turned half away in
case she should throw herself at me. Her face showed
distress at my apparent coldness but her first questions
were still of Anon. Was she all right? Would she be
happy and loved where she was? I assured Beth that
Anon would be worked, pampered and adored.

'Something's wrong,' she said. 'Is it just because the
local rag printed a few lines about you taking Anon to
America?'

'I didn't even know about it. How in hell did they
find out about that?'

'Not from any of us. What's wrong?' She looked
me in the eye. Sometimes it seemed that she was able
to read my mind. 'It's your arm again, isn't it?'

I gave her a big kiss and tried to pretend that my
shoulder was doing no more than nagging slightly after
the long plane-ride; but she soon had it out of me that I
had taken a fall. After that, there was no resisting her.

All that I wanted in the world was an enormous meal,
a bath, a shave and a sleep. There had been no breakfast
on the plane and I had been in my clothes for two days
and nights. Instead, I was forced into our car, which

seemed very old and drab all of a sudden, and whirled off to the hospital. The doctors confirmed my diagnosis, that I had torn the muscle again. They wanted to re-admit me but there was a *sotto voce* argument beyond the screens, of which I could hear enough to realise that the nursing staff had strong views on the subject. I could be treated as an outpatient but only over their collective dead bodies would I be admitted for anything short of a total headectomy.

I was sent home again with orders to rest. There are certain advantages in being a bad patient.

Isobel and Henry wanted to badger me with ques-tions about my trip but, beyond saying that the client had indeed been the widow, I made it clear that my lips were, for the moment, sealed. Beth supported me. I had promised, and that was that. I got to bed at last during the afternoon, thinking that I need never worry about being cuckolded. If Beth should ever fall from grace, she would undoubtedly, in her uncompromis-ing honesty, subject me to a stroke by stroke account of something which I would have preferred not to know.

Next morning I surfaced, feeling very fit provided, once again, that I did not attempt any movement of my left arm. At least jet lag was no problem. Three days and two nights of intermittent sleep had not been enough to set back my body-clock.

We slipped back into the same routine. Isobel and Beth continued to do all the real labour while I looked after the paperwork, taught kindergarten and saw any visitors. But for sudden jolts of pain I could have believed that Bubba and sudden death had been a dream, no more than the memory of a random thought.

But Jess Holbright had mentioned Lord Crail. Crail was a regular client. It was his sensible habit to vanish abroad soon after the shooting season ended, leaving

106

his dogs with us for much-needed retraining. I looked in the diary but he had not yet made a booking.

After some hesitation, I picked a moment when I had the sitting room to myself and telephoned him. I expected a long argument with his manservant, who considered me to belong among the tradesmen, but Crail himself answered the phone.

'Hello, John,' he said. I made an inarticulate noise. Lord Crail was rather less than my age and I knew him well enough to pull his leg or to tell him a blue joke, but although he always used my Christian name he had never invited me to use his. Luckily, he went on speaking. 'I was going to phone you. We thought that we wouldn't be able to get away this year, but Linda's aunt made a miraculous recovery. Or else the old bat was swinging the lead all along. Can you still take the dogs?'

'We'll be up to our backsides in pups before much longer, but we'll fit them in somewhere,' I said.

'That's fine. Day after tomorrow?'

'No problem.' I was about to mention the widow when I heard Beth in the kitchen. Beth would not deliberately eavesdrop, but if she happened to pick up the other extension to make a call I could hardly break off in mid-sentence. 'Can you bring them over yourself?'

'I usually do,' he pointed out.

He arrived two days later in his new Range Rover, immaculate in new tweeds. (Crail was permanently and notoriously broke but he managed a lifestyle to which I could never aspire, largely, one gathered, by playing one creditor off against another. But he usually paid our bills more or less on time.) He was accompanied by a Labrador and two spaniels. I met him at the door as Beth was leading away the dogs.

'I suppose you've been shooting rabbits over them again,' I said severely. 'Come on in.' I probably sounded like a wife greeting her husband on his return from the pub. Nothing unsteadies a dog like hunting rabbits for a lax owner.

'Don't knock it,' he said, smiling. 'It's your bread and butter. And there's no sport as much fun as rabbiting over dogs. I haven't the heart to check them, they enjoy it so much. If you happen to be blessed with four legs, chasing fur must be the nearest thing to heaven. You'll have them steady for me again before the grouse season opens. You always do.' He looked at my sling and my fading bruises. 'I heard that you'd been attacked. Are you on the mend?'

We fetched coffee. He carried the tray for me. We settled down in front of the fire in the sitting room. His mention of grouse had given me an opening. 'I don't know how you can afford to shoot grouse these days,' I said. 'You don't have any heather of your own.'

Crail is a cheerful young man and his face is usually split by a broad grin, but he nodded sombrely. 'Christless, isn't it? Of course, a good moor takes a hell of a lot of keeping and you have to cut down heavily on the number of sheep you can graze over it. All the same, I think that supply and demand have taken over. I only went once last year and I only managed that by renting a whole moor near Perth for a day and advertising for paying Guns.'

'And I'll bet you made a profit out of it,' I said.

His grin came back. 'Not quite. I couldn't cover my own costs out of what the others paid me. But I took Gus Brown along with the other beaters— '

'You swore to me that you'd never have him in the line again,' I broke in. 'You told me you wouldn't even let him beat a carpet.' Angus Brown was a notorious local poacher, a ferreter and an occasional and disreputable wildfowling guide. It was quite common for a landowner to find a party of visiting Italians shooting geese over his

108

potato or stubble fields under Gus's aegis and without the least shadow of permission.

'So I did,' Crail said. 'I'd found that he was going home with more pheasants than the guests and the game dealer put together. He has a bloody good dog.'

'I know,' I said. I had often regretted selling Gus the pup which had turned out to be one of the smartest spaniels around.

'We were paying thirty quid a bird between us. That meant that every bird shot and picked up cost us about four quid each. Any pricked birds that Gus got away with were birds we didn't have to pay for,' Crail said simply. 'And then the owners had wanted to send Horace along with us. "An extra Gun to share the cost," they said. Huh!'

'Fair comment,' I said. Horace – Sir Horace French – was a devastating shot at driven grouse. Landowners had been known to add him to a party of Guns, free of charge, for the sake of the increased bag.

'On an open moor, Gus didn't have quite the same scope for hiding a dead bird and going back for it later, but I knew that he was marking down any that he reckoned were pricked and which had been missed by the pickers-up. I could count on him going back over the moor by moonlight. And that dog of his wouldn't miss a thing. When he got home to his hovel, just before dawn, I was waiting for him. I relieved him of fourteen brace and got a damn good price from the dealer.'

'You're as big a crook as he is,' I said, trying to keep the amusement out of my voice.

'The bottom's dropping out of farming,' he said sadly. 'You can't afford to miss a trick these days, if your money's all tied up in the land. I'd sell some of it off, only I've left it too late.'

'Also, your pickers-up ought to be shot for missing so many.'

'I only took two pickers-up to serve the whole line. I was going to invite you and Beth along, but you were under the weather at the time. And Gus's birds didn't all have shot in them. As I said, that's a clever dog.'

Rather than risk moving again I asked Crail to pour more coffee. 'That must have been the occasion when you had an American couple along,' I said.

He put my cup where I could reach it without stretching. 'That's right. The man was the first to answer my advertisement. He only wanted one gun at that time, but he phoned me later wanting a second and I was able to fit his wife in. And how that lady could shoot driven birds!'

'Better than Sir Horace?' I asked.

'She started where he leaves off. Her husband said that she was red-hot at skeet and I believed him. I'd like to get her over here again,' Crail said wistfully, 'and match her against some of our gambling men. Then I could maybe afford to shoot grouse again this year. I had to send her with the beaters as a walking gun, to stop her pushing up the cost of the day too far. We were all getting worried. I remember that she seemed to get as much fun from working their spaniel as from the shooting. Just my kind of girl in fact!'

'What else do you remember about them?' I asked.

'Not a thing. It was about six months ago,' he pointed out. 'Why?'

'There's a strong possibility that he was the man whose body I found in the Eden.'

Crail looked at me in surprise for a few seconds. 'I thought that they'd identified that man as a crook.'

'They did,' I said.

I expected him to say that the man had not looked like a crook, but Crail's mind tended to follow other tracks. 'He paid his whack. Or, rather, she did. In traveller's

110

cheques, as I remember. Why would they spend good money on grouse shooting while he had a good scam going? The two things seem incompatible somehow.'

'Even conmen need a little relaxation,' I said.

'I suppose so. Wasn't that his wife? Don't tell me that she was in it with him?'

'That was his wife, and I think she'd come over to try and persuade him to turn over a new leaf.'

'If I were not a happily married man,' Crail said, 'I'd rush over to the States and pay court to the widow. All that charm and money too. So that was the same spaniel that you took to the States? There was something in the local paper about it. "Murder victim's dog flies out." That sort of guff.'

I wasted several minutes in trying to stimulate his recollection of the American couple but it was only when I asked whether they had seemed to know any of the other Guns that his memory produced anything new.

'They didn't know any others in the party,' he said. 'I had to introduce them around. But . . . ' He fell silent.

'But?' I said hopefully.

'But, yes. It's only an impression, mind. But after one of the drives, the second I think, when the beaters arrived at the butts, I got the impression that Gus Brown knew the man. It was no more than a nod and a couple of words.'

'Couldn't it have been something like "Good shooting, sir"?'

'Possible,' Crail said slowly. 'Just possible, although Gus Brown doesn't usually go in for these little courtesies. I certainly thought that it looked more like "So we meet again!" or "Up yours, Charlie." Neither of them was looking too pleased to see the other. But it was a nothing, over and finished in less than a second.'

I only noticed because I was keeping an eye on Gus. They seemed to avoid each other after that. Should I tell the police about it?'

The police would undoubtedly want to know how Lord Crail had come to realise that his guest was the man who had come floating to our feet on the Eden several months later; and I had no wish to be questioned further until Jessica Holbright had made her escape from Texas.

'I wouldn't bother,' I said. 'I'll pass the word on when the time seems right. Your impression that the American had bumped into Gus in the past doesn't mean a lot, unless Gus had seen him in the company of the man they're still looking for.'

'He'd probably hired Gus as a wildfowling guide at some time.'

'But not necessarily alone. Do you know Gus well enough to find out from him?'

Crail forced a sardonic laugh. 'You've got to be joking,' he said. 'Gus doesn't take kindly to being beaten at his own game. He hates my guts. And he's such a spiteful beggar that I told Mr Wallace to watch out for him. Wallace caught him sneaking around one of the farms.'

Mr Wallace, Lord Crail's keeper, was a former warrant officer in the Scots Guards. Crail would certainly get no favours from Gus Brown.

'I'd better see him myself,' I said.

'And the best of British luck to you,' Lord Crail said. 'Stand well back and try not to catch anything off him.'

After one painful attempt I decided that I could not manage the car's manual gear-change for myself. Henry was away on an overnight visit to his niece in Oban. Beth and Isobel each refused to chauffeur me on the grounds that, one, they were too busy, two, I wasn't fit to travel and, three, who on earth would call on Gus Brown if they didn't have to? My lips still being sealed I could not argue.

There was, however, an alternative. Gus was either too mean, too broke or too used to operating on a shoestring to own a telephone, but it was widely known that messages left for him at his local pub would reach him, and with remarkable promptness except when his credit had run out. He must have been in funds that week but in need of work, because I phoned the pub that morning and Gus arrived the same afternoon.

The day was wet but warm, so I had made an excuse to take several young pups into the barn for some elementary humanising and training. This was partly in expectation of Gus's arrival. Beth would have been furious if I had taken him into the house. Not only was he notoriously light-fingered but his arrival was usually marked by a gust of beer-fumes overlying certain less forgivable personal odours.

Gus stood in the barn's wide doorway, glowering at me, the epitome of male scruffiness. He reminded me strongly of Jess Holbright's description of Bubba. It was all there – the beard, in his case trimmed to a ragged fringe around his round face, a spare tyre bulging over the belt of his jeans, even the grubby plimsolls; but he was wearing a crumpled tweed hat instead of the giveaway baseball cap and a donkey jacket over his workshirt. He had loose lips and eyes like gas bubbles on a swamp.

I called the pups to me. There was only one canvas chair in the barn and I was damned if I was getting out of it, especially for Gus. I pointed to one of the straw bales which serve as hiding places for planted dummies and invited him to sit on that.

He sat down heavily. His eyes went from my sling to

my face. 'I heard you'd been in the wars,' he said. It was a flat statement, not intended to convey sympathy. 'What's this you want doing?' My message had hinted at casual employment. Outside the shooting season, Gus would have had no objection to continuing his poaching. His market soon dried up, however, so he turned his hand, quite competently, to doing odd jobs for anybody who was prepared to risk petty theft or fleas.

As it happened, I wanted a new water-pipe laid to the kennels and two new kennels and runs erected. Gus would do the work well and more cheaply than any contractor; and the human flea does not readily transfer to dogs. While I outlined the work I was wondering how to approach the other subject. The pups had settled down in a snoring huddle beside my chair.

When I had finished, Gus nodded brusquely. 'Right,' he said. 'When do you want me to make a start?'

'The materials are on order. I'll let you know when they're here. But first,' I said, 'I want you to tell me something.'

He looked at me in silence. Giving away information was not in Gus's nature.

'What do you know about the American?' I asked.

'Which American?' he retorted. I could tell from his little dark eyes that he knew the answer to his own question; he was being contrary on principle, or wondering what *quid pro quo* he could extract.

I had hoped to avoid mentioning the thorny subject of Lord Crail's grouse-shoot. 'There was an American shooting near Perth,' I said circumspectly. 'You were among the beaters. You seemed to know him.'

He bristled. 'Who told you that? It was yon bogger Crail.'

'It doesn't matter who told me. There was an American there and you spoke to him.'

'Never saw him before. Never in my life. I just telled

114

him that his woman had a bird down behind him and he'd best send the wee dog.'

Gus was avoiding my eye. Moreover, if he had seen a bird down and unpicked he would have kept the information to himself. He slipped a hand under his donkey jacket for a good scratch.

'I think you'd met him before,' I said.

'You calling me a fleggar to my face?'

He got up to go, a picture of injured dignity. The light from one of the high windows fell on his face. 'You've got the remains of a shiner beside your left eye,' I said. 'About the same vintage as mine. Did I put it there?'

He sat down again slowly. 'Dinna' ken what you mean.'

Did I remember, from before I was stabbed, a sudden waft of body odour? I could not be sure. But it seemed unlikely that any foul deeds had been committed in northern Fife without Gus's knowledge if not his active participation. Such at least was the strength of his reputation. The bluff seemed worth following up anyway. 'You know damn well,' I said. 'Somebody came here to steal the American's dog. Before he stabbed me, I caught him a clout across the face.'

With a visible effort, he met my eye. 'Not me,' he said.

'I could say that it was.'

'Just you do that. I never laid finger on you. I mind reading about it in the papers. I was in a cell that night, drunk and disorderly. And you can do your ain fockin' work.' He got up again and stamped towards the doorway.

His bluster did nothing to convince me of his innocence but his flat denial left me, for the moment, weaponless. Gus accepted harassment from the police as philosophically as he accepted his fleas. It came to

115

me that there was another area in which he might be vulnerable. 'Where's Nella?' I asked him.

The mention of his spaniel stopped him in his tracks. 'What's it to you?' he demanded.

'You never paid me for her,' I said.

'I did so!' he said.

But I could see doubt on his face. Gus was known for never settling up if it could possibly be avoided, and I was sure that he had lost track of the innumerable debts which he had left behind him in a paperchase of unpaid bills and solicitors' letters. It was a pity, I thought, that he and Lord Crail could not get on together; they had such a lot in common. 'You have a receipt?' I asked him.

'I'd never have asked it. There's no need of papers between honest men.' He gave me a look of hurt dignity.

'I'm thinking of repossessing her,' I said.

He came back and stood over me. 'You'd never!' His voice had gone up to a squeal.

He was absolutely right. I was bluffing. As Crail had said, Gus was spiteful; and the kennels were vulnerable. 'Try me,' I said.

He was thinking hard. Gus was cast in the same mould as David Conrad Falconer. If he was capable of affection it was for his dog and his ferrets. 'I'll do your bloody work,' he said at last. 'You can take it off that.'

'With interest at ten per cent per month for four years?' I said. 'I think I'd rather have the dog. Tell me about the American. Surely it can't hurt you, for once, to pass the word along. Or do you have a good reason for keeping quiet?'

He thought again and then made a gesture of surrender. 'There's no reason,' he said. 'I just can't thole being pushed. I'll tell you. I'd met him the once, on Wester Gunnet Farm. He came on me suddenly using the ferrets. I told him I'd the farmer's leave to ferret

116

there but he wouldna' ha'e it. An' he was richt,' Gus added with unusual candour. 'He chased me off the place. So, when I saw him shooting at the muircocks, I thought I'd just have a wee word.'

'I can guess what that word was,' I said. 'Were those the only times you ever saw him?'

Gus hesitated once more, balancing my threat against the engrained habit of secrecy for secrecy's sake. 'I see'd him just the once more,' he said at last. 'I went to the Tay afore dawn, below Newburgh, for a crack at the geese. But when the birds came off the water there was two men in the reeds I'd not known was there. They took two for four shots and turned the birds back. I was well hid. I bided where I was and they walked past without seeing me. It was the Yank and another chiel and their twa dogs. But they left o'er soon,' Gus added with satisfaction, 'for the best of the flight came later.'

'What did the other man look like?'

'Two penn'orth of nothing,' Gus said contemptuously. 'Skinny. A poor creature, like yourself. He'd a fore-and-aft hat pulled down against the wind, but what I could see of his face was nipped. If he'd been a yowe in a sale, I'd not have bid for him. And if there was anything else about him, I never saw it.'

I knew that there was something else that I should ask but it eluded me. 'All right, Gus,' I said. 'We're all square now. And you can still do the work if you want to.'

'I'll think about it,' he said. He stooped over me. One of the pups woke up and nosed his leg but was ignored. I was too late in recognising the fury in his eyes. Suddenly, he punched my shoulder. '*Now* we're all square,' he said.

I nursed myself for ten minutes before I could wipe my eyes and make a move. The pups sat round, watching me and wondering. They had never before heard the sounds which a man can make when pain is beyond bearing.

Eight

Beth could see that my shoulder was giving me trouble, but there are no meters for measuring pain. For all that she knew, I might have been feeling sorrier for myself rather than suffering more. She left me to slump in one of the fireside chairs in the kitchen while she uncomplainingly lugged feed and water, cleaned runs and exercised dogs.

I was in a state of indecision. Any word from me to the police might start the hue and cry which Jess Holbright dreaded. But Gus Brown was on the loose, probably the only person knowingly to have seen the late Mr Holbright with his elusive friend.

How, I wondered, had Gus known exactly where to land his punch? My sling would have suggested no more than that somewhere around the left arm or chest would be vulnerable; but he had thumped his first right on to the wound itself. Chance? Or had he in truth been my night-time assailant? If the latter, then he must have made contact with the second man and been hired to steal Anon. In which case, was the description which he had given me a pure fabrication? Or was there another player in the game?

In bed the following morning, I decided that Jess Holbright would have to take her chance.

Beth went out to feed the pups and then came back to help me dress myself. My shoulder had begun to settle down once more and felt little worse than it had before

Gus's attempt at therapy but from time to time, at any incautious movement, it sent me a warning. Enough, it said, was enough.

'There was a message for you,' Beth said as she worked my shirtsleeve carefully up my left arm. 'It was from Mr Rodgers's office. But I couldn't understand it at all. It was something about spring being here at last. I said that spring might only just have arrived in Glasgow but that it had been spring here weeks ago. They said to tell you anyway. Do you know what it means?'

I felt a wave of relief, slightly damped by the knowledge of a difficult interview to come. 'Yes,' I said. 'I know exactly what it means and I'm glad to hear it. It means that I'm free to tell Sergeant Ewell about my trip.'

'And me,' she said. She finished tucking my shirt in and knelt to tie my laces.

'And you, when the time's ripe. Would you phone the Sergeant and tell him that I have some information for him? Thank you, darling, I can manage from here,' I added.

'I'll do that.' She looked at me appraisingly. 'You look a bittie brighter this morning. You were gey peely-wally last night.' The phrase took me back. It had been a favourite with my mother. Beth used it self-deprecatingly. Usually, she avoided the Scots tongue, trying to speak perfect English although with a sweet trace of a Fife accent. She had, as she once admitted, a misguided idea that I would love her more if she 'lived up to me', whatever that might mean. There was more need for me to live up to her brave spirit and eternal patience.

The Sergeant came soon after I had finished my breakfast. Henry, back from his visit to Oban, had walked over with Isobel and, although Henry's help with the chores would have been appreciated and he

119

would have been happy to give it, I asked him to join me with the Sergeant in the sitting room. The Sergeant was not going to be pleased with me and I felt a need for the support of an older and wiser head.

Beth had lit the fire in the sitting room. The central heating kept the room warm but the fire, as usual, transformed it from a gloomy and old-fashioned cavern, only redeemed by the painting over the mantelpiece, into something cosy and comforting. I took a little time settling us into chairs and adding a log to the fire while I wondered how to express myself. The message and the Sergeant had come at me in a rush.

'You'll remember,' I said at last, 'that you agreed to the sale of the spaniel to a firm of Glasgow solicitors.'

The Sergeant's friendly posture shifted slightly. 'That dratted dog!' he said. 'We must have had six or seven enquiries for her after her photo was in the paper. It wasn't even a photo of the same dog – even I could tell that.'

I took craven advantage of the diversion. 'How did the paper get to know that I'd taken her abroad?' I asked.

'I wondered the same myself. I asked the editor. He told me that you were spotted at Prestwick. That's all he'd say.'

'Just an ill chance,' I said. 'The solicitors were acting for a client in the States. I was hired, under a promise of strictest confidentiality, to deliver the dog. When I got out there, I was met by a woman who I guessed was the widow of the dead owner.'

The Sergeant looked up sharply from his notebook. 'How sure are you?'

'She confirmed it. That put me in a spot. As I said, I had given my promise to maintain confidentiality. But she admitted that she intended to vanish because, although she assured me that she had never touched any of her husband's fraudulent profits, the authorities and others were looking for her on the assumption that she was holding the kitty.

'I didn't want to break my word. But neither did I want any information to be lost if it would be of any help to you. The best I could think of was to get her to talk freely to me by promising to remain silent until I received a message that I was free to speak. That message reached me this morning.'

'Then you'd better speak,' said the Sergeant. He was no longer the mild and approachable man with whom I had been establishing a rapport. He frowned at his notebook and there was a grittiness in his voice which suggested that I was in for a tongue-lashing at the very least. For the moment, he wanted as much as I would give him willingly.

'You already know that she came over to visit her husband early last autumn,' I said. 'Her intention, she told me, was to persuade him to come home and turn over a new leaf. But she failed.'

'And you believed her?' the Sergeant asked.

'I did. She never met the other man, the one you're looking for. But she and her husband planned to attend a shoot organised by Lord Crail.'

'The lady was shooting?' The Sergeant sounded surprised. Lady shots are much less common in Scotland than they are in Texas.

'By all accounts, she's damned good with a shotgun,' I said. I tried not to remember that she was more than good with a pistol. 'But she didn't have a gun. Her husband phoned his friend who brought over a rather distinctive gun, a sixteen-bore sidelock of Italian make. She only saw this man from her bedroom window. She was looking down from above but she described him as having a round head, a chest like a barrel and protruding ears.' I paused. What else had Jess said? 'Brown hair

121

parted on the left and no bald spot. I think that was all that I got from the widow but—'

'Just haud a wee,' said the Sergeant. 'Where did this discussion take place?'

I did not know the name of the ranch but I could have provided enough information to pinpoint it on the map. On the other hand, I had no intention of placing myself in the area where Bubba had been shot, nor of dropping young Jim in the mire. 'Overnight, in a lounge at Houston airport,' I said. And if anyone cared to assume that I meant the main airport of Houston rather than the alternative Hobby airport, that would be their fault rather than mine.

'Describe the woman.'

'Tall. Nearly my height,' I said. 'Perhaps five-nine or ten. Early to middle thirties. A good figure. Her hair is probably light brown but bleached to a sort of dusky blonde by the sun. Good features but with a strong, square jaw. The sun hasn't done her skin any favours. That's about all I noticed. You probably got a better description from Mrs Blagdon at the hotel.'

The Sergeant nodded. 'We did. But what I wanted to know was whether your description matched hers. And it does. What name did she give you?'

'She wouldn't give me a name,' I said. A name would have completed the chain which still linked me to the now defunct Bubba.

The Sergeant looked pained. 'Go on. You were going to tell me something else.'

'Lord Crail came to leave his dogs with us,' I said, picking my words with care. 'He was about to go abroad. I didn't have leave to speak to you at the time, so I thought it best to ask him about the occasion when the American couple attended his shoot. He hadn't noticed much about them except that one of the beaters passed

122

a few words with the man in a way that suggested that they'd met before.'

'Who was the beater? Perhaps I'd better have a word with Lord Crail.'

'He's probably in Spain by now,' I said. 'But I can tell you who the beater was. Gus Brown.'

'If we're talking about the same Gus Brown,' said the Sergeant, 'that's a real skellum.'

'Then we're talking about the same one,' I said. I nerved myself and went on. 'I had a word with him yesterday.'

The Sergeant threw down his notebook and glared at me as if he could hardly believe his ears. 'You . . . did . . . what?' The last word came out as a yelp.

'I spoke to Gus Brown.'

'Really, Mr Cunningham,' said the Sergeant, 'I thought better of you. I can just understand that you felt bound by the promise which you'd given to the lady and thought that it outweighed your duty to the police, although my superiors may not agree. If Lord Crail was about to journey abroad, I suppose that you did little harm in speaking to him. But to take it on yourself to interrogate a . . . a skybal of a man who might be a suspect for all you knew or cared— '

The Sergeant's voice was rising higher in his per-turbation. Henry, who had listened in intent silence, cut through it. 'Think for a moment, Sergeant,' he said. He spoke softly but with an authority that the Sergeant seemed to recognise. 'By promising to remain silent until told that he could speak, Mr Cunningham obtained information which could be of use to you. Rather than break faith with his informant, he kept his word. He must have known that this would leave him open to your annoyance. His easiest course would have been to let you remain in the dark. You would never have known that you had any cause for complaint. Instead,

123

rightly or wrongly, he took his information-gathering a little further while he waited for the all-clear. Before you decide whether his actions hindered the police in the execution of their duty, hadn't you better hear what those actions were and what he found out?'

'Thank you, Henry,' I said. I tried to think of a suitable reward. 'Would you like a drink?'

'I hope that you didn't waste your time asking Gus Brown such silly questions,' Henry said. 'A beer will do for the moment. But don't stop asking me. You can tempt me with something a little stronger later on. I'll get it,' he added, shooting up to his considerable height. 'And you?'

I looked at the Sergeant but he shook his head as though repelling a persistent fly. 'Too early for me,' I said. 'Perhaps I'll join you later, if Sergeant Ewell hasn't eaten me.'

Henry sat down and poured beer for himself.

The diversion had given the Sergeant time to reflect. 'Very well,' he said. 'Tell me about your interview with Gus Brown.'

'He had had words with the American when they met on Wester Gunnet Farm, where Gus was using ferrets without permission.'

The Sergeant nodded. 'We knew that Wester Gunnet was one of the farms he shot over. At least we got that far. Nobody introduced him, he saw the pigeon on the kale as he was passing by so he knocked on the farmer's door. He never had company there, so far as we know.'

'The two men must have been careful not to be seen together,' I said. 'Walking over farmland, you think you're alone but there are eyes on you. Just lift a gun to anything you're not permitted to shoot and the farmer appears like a genie out of a bottle. They seem to have limited their joint shooting expeditions to dawn flights on the foreshore. That's where Gus saw the two of them together – on the Tay, near Newburgh. The American was with a man who Gus said was small and very lean. He was wearing a hat so Gus didn't see his hair. Gus said that he was a poor-looking creature. Like me, he said.'

'Dodsakes!' said the Sergeant. 'That's three different descriptions you've brought us. Did the man have a dog with him?'

That, I realised, was the question which had been evading my mind. 'Gus mentioned a dog. He didn't describe it and I forgot to ask him. And I can only pass on what I'm told,' I said.

'I ken that fine.' The Sergeant considered his notes. 'Even if Gus was telling the truth for once in his misbegotten life, there's no saying that that wasn't the one time that the American went out with some other acquaintance. On the other hand, Gus could be hand in glove with the other man and lying his head off.'

'I don't think so,' I said. 'I had to twist his arm to get him to tell me anything.' As soon as the words were out, I wanted to call them back. I knew that I had let something drop. Too late, I tried to scrape earth over it. 'It was because I was distracted by the bickering that I forgot to ask about the dog.' I wanted to go on, to drag the discussion a long way away, but my mind had dried up.

'Is . . . that . . . so?' said the Sergeant. 'Just what exactly did you say to him?'

'I threatened to tell you that he was the man who attacked me,' I said. 'He had the remains of a shiner and when I thought about it I was almost sure that I had smelled his distinctive odour just before I was stabbed. Almost but not quite. That didn't seem to bother him too much – he said that he was locked up for D and D at the time – so then I pointed out that he'd never paid me for his pup and I threatened to take her back. That shook him.'

125

'Likely so,' the Sergeant said grimly. 'Either way, you've done just the wrongest thing you could think of. If it was Gus who attacked you, then he is indeed hand in glove with the other man, in which case he's either told you a fairytale or run to warn him. If not, you've very likely put the idea of blackmail into his head; and it does not seem to me that the unknown man would take blackmail lightly. If Angus Brown turns up floating in the Tay or the Eden, you'll be responsible. You didn't think of that?'

I held my tongue. I had already said too much.

'I don't suppose that he did,' Henry said. 'And I don't think that you need do so either. To say the least, you're howling before you're hurt. You'll probably find Gus going about his usual insanitary business.'

'That's possible,' the Sergeant said more mildly. 'Well, well. I'll say no more until we know, one way or the other. I'll let my superiors know about all this. No doubt there will be more questions. But if you meant to do me a favour, you've missed the mark.'

Henry managed a smile. 'The days have gone by when the bearer of bad news was put to death,' he said.

'That's all you know,' the Sergeant said bitterly. But Henry jollied and coaxed and soothed him and he was preparing to take his leave in a slightly less hostile mood when the door was opened by Beth. Her usually calm young face bore the look of one who has taken just so much and will not take any more.

'Did you know,' she began, 'that a whole hutch of ferrets has appeared, down by the gate. And if you think I'm having anything to do with the evil-looking little devils, you're on the wrong track. This note was with them.'

I took the note and read it aloud.

Mr Cunningham you bastert,

                    I got to go away for a bit and it's your faut. So you can mynd my foumarts until I get back.

Yours respeckfully, Angus Brown.

For a day or two I cringed at each ring of the doorbell, expecting at any moment an influx of furious police officers, but it never came. It was as though the police, huffy at my interference and at my dilatoriness in passing on my information, had made up their minds that they could manage without my help, so there!

I was happy enough to forget the whole blasted business. I had done my wellmeaning best in difficult circumstances, had probably spoiled the Sergeant's chances of promotion and had got my fingers justly rapped. From now on, I would be a convenient target of blame for every calamity or hiccup in the investigation. I preferred not to think about any of it. We seemed to be entering another period during which nothing would happen to disturb the placid routine of our days.

My mind, if nobody else's, was eased by a phone-call from Gus Brown. It came from a public phone at some distance, to judge from the coins which I heard drop. The gist of the call was mainly abusive, but he did enquire anxiously after his ferrets. He probably knew that I would never willingly destroy any animal except those which were a nuisance to man, or for food, but he caught me at the wrong moment and said the wrong things. My shoulder was paining me and I was ever more sure that Gus had been my assailant. I told him that I had drowned his blasted ferrets in a bucket and that, given half a chance, I would do the same for him. And I hung up, feeling better.

In fact, I rather enjoyed having the ferrets around.

Beth at first refused to go near them, so Henry and I took over their keeping. We would have liked to have worked them, but the few rabbits still on the ground were breeding already so that the season for ferreting was over. We fed them on the dried mince which went into the dogs' diets and they thrived.

When Beth realised that well-kept ferrets were very tame with man (and that they have no smell if prevented from carrying surplus food into their sleeping quarters) she fell for their kittenish charm and took over their management. The old hob was a particularly friendly creature and enjoyed riding around on her shoulder. He travelled many miles in that way, because it is no bad thing to accustom young gundogs to the presence of ferrets.

I had written out an account of Gus's phone-call and posted it to Sergeant Ewell for onward transmission. This brought no immediate reaction and I wondered whether the police had written it off as a fabrication on my part. This seemed unlikely. They would surely realise that any such invention would prove damning if Gus were to turn out to have been dead all along. It occurred to me that I was probably suspected already of having done away with him. The implications of that thought became too complex for my comfort and I pushed it to the back of my mind.

But a few days later, Sergeant Ewell turned up again. The day was bright and the countryside trying to fool mankind with signs that spring was on the way towards becoming summer. My shoulder was on the mend. I could still not tolerate the kick of a shotgun but I could use the dummy launcher in a peculiar, back-handed way, so I had been allowed by my nannies – as I called them, to their great annoyance – to take a quartet of year-old dogs to The Moss for some advanced lessons. Wildflowers were rife, a thrush was singing and I was for the moment unaware of my shoulder. I felt almost euphoric – until I saw the Sergeant picking his way across the rough ground.

I was in the middle of one of my most testing series of exercises – to sit the dogs, walk on out of sight, fire several dummies into cover, whistle up the dogs and direct each of them on to one of the dummies while the others sat tight. It was not an occasion for distractions; young dogs are impetuous and one breach of discipline could set training back a week. I held up a hand in the gesture with which he would have stopped the traffic and he waited patiently, a black sentinel beside a stunted pine, until the dummies were gathered in.

We met near the small pond, beside a tree which had been felled by the winds of winter. I sat the dogs and seated myself on the trunk. The Sergeant preferred to stand. His manner was aloof and mildly censorious as though I were an erring child, not yet forgiven.

'I passed your letter on up the line,' he said.

'But you don't believe me?'

'Oh, I think I believe you,' he said. 'But then, I start from the assumption that you may be misguided but are telling the truth. I can't speak for my superiors. However, it seems that Gus Brown's ramshackle old van has been seen near Edinburgh, driven by a man answering his description. The number-plates had been changed and by the time the penny dropped the van was gone. Your letter said only that the call had come from a call-box at "some distance". Could it have been from Edinburgh?'

'It could,' I said. 'Or from almost anywhere else.'

He frowned austerely. Obviously, in his view I wasn't trying. 'Do you remember the tones when the coins dropped?'

'Not with any certainty. And if I did it wouldn't help you, because I've only a vague idea of the interval of time before the pips went and he had to put some more money in.'

He satisfied himself that I was not holding back any vital fragments of information and then gave a sigh. 'We think that he may be living rough in the back of his van, somewhere in the Central Belt, and taking casual farm or keepering work. He must have more on his conscience than a little poaching.'

'Like putting a knife into me?' I suggested.

'M'hm, perhaps. If we could only put our hands on the man! You should never have taken it on yourself to question him.'

The feelings of guilt had faded and I was beginning to be irritated. 'There's a limit to how often I can say I'm sorry. What more do you want? I passed on the description Gus gave me.'

'Aye. Both words of it. And was he telling the truth? You of all people should have thought to ask about the mannie's dog.'

We were sheltered from the breeze and I was too warm in the sun. I took off my coat and spread it over the treetrunk. 'Sit down and relax for a moment,' I said. 'Or else go away. I made a guess as to what I should do and I guessed wrong. They can hardly blame you for my stupidity.'

He looked suspiciously at the lining of my coat to be sure that it was clean and then seated himself carefully. 'Aye they can,' he said. 'It was on my recommendation that the springer bitch was let go.'

'If she'd been kept in hiding or put down, you'd never have known that Gus Brown knew anything at all,' I pointed out.

'Try telling that to the super,' he said bitterly. 'And here's one inspector due to retire and another's applied for transfer to the Serious Crime Squad. When those places are filled, there'll be no more vacancies for years.'

I headed him back towards the main topic before he could become too caught up with his own troubles. 'Surely they can find the "other man" among his business contacts?'

He was in no mood for looking on bright sides. 'They're sure it's nobody that he met officially. They're looking hard at the staff of all the banks, because the money disappeared too smoothly for him to have managed it without help, but there's thousands of them. Just thousands, some of them the kind of men who play golf with the Scottish Secretary. And never a sign of that girl who called herself Miss McGillivray, although they've looked and looked.'

'Difficult,' I said with as much sympathy as I could put into my voice.

'Aye.' He threw a pebble into the small pond and watched the ripples dancing in the sunlight. 'I'm on your side, mind. But there are those who're beginning to wonder about you.'

'They can wonder all they want,' I said. 'I've told nothing but the truth.'

'So I hope.' He hummed a dirgelike tune and threw another pebble. 'I'll tell you one thing,' he said suddenly. 'Gus Brown's alibi doesn't stand up. He spent part of that night in a cell sure enough, but he wasn't picked up until an hour after the attack on you. He had fresh marks of violence on his face.'

'That's good, isn't it?' I said. 'From my point of view, I mean.'

'Maybe, maybe not. He was in a brawl when he was arrested. But say that he was your attacker and look at it from the Chief Inspector's viewpoint. Gus Brown attacks you because of the wee dog. Next thing, you've fetched her out of the country. Then you have a wee word with Gus and he vanishes. And we've nobody's word but yours to explain what's going on. And you

131

don't give us an explanation that explains anything.'

'Because I don't have one. Somebody has to know something.' I cast around in my mind. 'What about the landlady at the pub?' I said. 'The one who takes Gus's messages. Doesn't she know anything?'

He shrugged. 'She didn't listen to the few calls that he got, or so she said. She remembered you leaving a message for him. And once, she says, a mannie phoned and caught Gus in the bar. She heard him say "But who the hell are you?" and then "How can I be sure I get paid?" That was all and she can't even be sure which day it was. It could have been anything. Any damned thing.'

We sat in silence, trying to enjoy the warmth of the sun and the sights and sounds and smells of a new spring, but his depression had infected me.

'I could bide here all day,' he said suddenly, 'rather than go back to the station. But needs must. Before I go, though, could I see you give one of the dogs a blind retrieve again? Damn't, that was a sight to see!'

Nine

The case had died out of the newspapers. We got on with our lives. Aurora presented us with eight fresh pups to worry about. Five young dogs reached the age for advanced training, ready to be sold for the next shooting season. I recovered my mobility and spent long hours in the fresh air, training variously aged classes or helping Beth and Isobel with the constant workload.

When I thought about the case at all, I decided that it had been relegated to the files of unsolved murders, never forgotten but never acted on unless some fresh facts should offer themselves.

I was wrong. The police came again, without warning and this time in strength – three of them in two cars, the first swinging in through the gates so sharply that Henry, who had walked over for his morning beer and a stint of work, had to jump aside. Sergeant Ewell, following more decorously in his panda car, made an apologetic face at him.

I was on my way back from the kennels to the house. Chief Inspector Ainslie emerged from the leading car and waited for me at the front door. 'A word in private,' he said sternly. 'I have some questions to ask you. You may have a solicitor present if you wish.'

My mouth dried immediately. This sounded serious. The Chief Inspector's manner had changed from that of a polite if curt civil servant to that of a headmaster about to deal severely with an erring pupil or the Colonel when I had once overstayed my leave. However often I assured myself that policemen are my friends, there was always a certain awe of those entrusted with the power of the law.

The few solicitors of my acquaintance flicked through my mind but there was not one whom I would willingly employ to do more than convey a house or draft a will. Except perhaps Mr Rodgers in distant Glasgow, and he would probably turn me away because of the possible conflict of interests.

'That won't be necessary,' I said. I nearly added that I had nothing to hide before I remembered that for once in my life it would have been untrue. 'I'd like Mr Kitts to be present. I trust his advice.'

Henry, puffing slightly, had arrived in time to hear my last words. He nodded briefly.

'Very well,' said the Chief Inspector. 'Shall we go inside or would you rather come to the nearest station?' Without waiting for an answer, he beckoned to the uniformed constable who was sitting to attention in the driving seat.

I led the way into the sitting room and annexed the two most comfortable chairs for myself and Henry, leaving the officers to stand or to find seats as they wished. Two could play at being uncompromising. The constable produced a notebook and took a chair beside the window. His two superiors sat on the settee, as far apart as space permitted.

The Chief Inspector produced a sheet of paper and studied it, either to refresh his memory or to gain time to formulate his first question. 'I have looked back over your earlier statements,' he said at last. 'Do you wish to modify any of them?'

'Certainly not,' I said irritably. 'I've told you nothing

but the absolute, literal truth.' With a few minor reservations, I added to myself.

'Take your time,' he said. 'Think about it.'

I could feel, literally, the hackles rising on the back of my neck. 'I don't need to think about it,' I said.

'You should. We now have a witness whose statement contradicts almost every word you have said.'

'He's lying,' I snapped.

The Chief Inspector half smiled. He had heard that argument before. 'Perhaps. Or perhaps not. You're a shooting man?'

'Yes,' I said.

'And a wildfowler?'

'I've already said so,' I pointed out. 'I was wildfowling when we found the body.'

'Do you still claim that you never met Mr Falconer while he was alive?'

'To the best of my knowledge,' I said.

The Chief Inspector paused like a terrier preparing to pounce on a rat. 'Fresh information suggests that you are one of the men we've been looking for all this time. The shooting companion.'

The suggestion was so unexpected that it took me several seconds to become angry. I felt myself about to explode, but Henry spoke first. 'Take it easy, John,' he said. 'We know that somebody's lying his head off, but the Chief Inspector has no way of knowing it as surely as we do. He has to follow up whatever statements he's given. Let's consider it calmly. I understood, Chief Inspector, that in view of the very smooth disappearance of the money you were searching for a confederate among the banking fraternity.'

'We were and we still are, but without success – not surprisingly, when you consider that virtually all the information that we had to go on, the three conflicting descriptions, the sixteen-bore shotgun and so on and so forth, all reached us through Mr Cunningham – the man who found the body and spirited away the dog.'

He made the last few words sound ominous. I was about to object that both actions had been perfectly innocent but I saw that, behind Henry's worn-out face, his keen brain was sifting the facts and inferences. I still had a lurking sense of guilt. Whatever I said would be wrong and possibly dangerous. I decided to hang fire.

'You said "one of the men",' Henry pointed out.

The Chief Inspector hesitated and then decided to put some more cards on the table. 'So far, we've been unable to find anybody in the banking fraternity who fits the pattern of the shooting companion. We were already becoming convinced that the late Mr Falconer may have had more than one associate. One expert who helped with the financial side and is now lying very low. And a friend who went shooting with him and who may or may not have been implicated in the fraud. Because that friend has not come forward, it's reasonable to suppose that he must have something on his conscience. One theory is that he killed Mr Falconer as a means towards getting away with some or all of the money.'

I found it impossible to believe that this was being said but Henry took it calmly and weighed his words. 'If you consider for a moment,' he said, 'I think you'll see that Mr Cunningham can hardly have been the shooting friend. For one thing, he is almost never outside the ken of his partners and myself.'

'You'd swear to that?'

The folds of Henry's face registered a sort of grim amusement. 'If you're hinting that we can only support Mr Cunningham by implicating ourselves, save your breath. Yes, we would swear to it.'

'He can hardly be in your sight all the time,' the Chief Inspector said.

'Of course not. But his activities are an open book

to us. He is here for most of every day. When he goes out, he is taking dogs to train on The Moss and brings them back within an hour or two. Or else he takes the car to fetch supplies or to deliver a dog and returns on schedule and with the errand accomplished. There is simply no margin for a secret life. But perhaps you're working round to the suggestion that an alibi given by his partners and his senior partner's husband is of little worth; that, in fact, we are acting as his willing accomplices for a share in the stolen money? A court wouldn't readily believe in such a wholesale conspiracy among respectable business people.'

'The suggestion was yours,' said the Chief Inspector, 'not mine.' He glanced towards the constable's moving pen.

'You had already made the implication,' Henry said patiently. 'Let's look at it from another angle. You are discounting the whole of Mr Cunningham's evidence on the word of one other man and a few vague deductions. But if Mr Cunningham was regularly lying to you, he would not have been so foolish as to give you three descriptions which could have been of three totally different men. Angus Brown, on the other hand— '

'I never mentioned that name,' the Chief Inspector said sharply.

'You didn't have to. Obviously, you've picked up Gus Brown, the one man we know of who has a strong motive to focus your attention on somebody else, rather than to admit that he made the attack on Mr Cunningham – which could land him on a charge of attempted murder.'

I opened my mouth but the Chief Inspector spoke first. 'Even discounting the description which Mr Cunningham said that he got from Angus Brown— '

'No,' Henry said. 'Don't do that. Those could be the only true words spoken by Gus. I dare say that he's changed his story now. But I think that we can reconcile the three descriptions which John passed along to you.'

The Chief Inspector sat back. 'This I have got to hear,' he said.

'Very well. Take first the wife's description. It seems to be of a totally different man. Well, considering the care which Mr Falconer had taken never to be seen with confederate in public, can you imagine the confederate driving up to the hotel in daylight and conferring with him outside the front door and under the bedroom windows? I suggest that the gun would have been conveyed by some trusted third party.

'The spurious Miss McGillivray described a tall man with fair hair. Gus Brown didn't see his hair but described him as small. But the lady was not who she pretended to be and she was in search of the dog. So she had some part in the mystery. In so far as the two descriptions can be compared, they seem to be exact opposites. I suggest that she used the occasion to plant a false description. And since she added that he had a deep voice and a Glasgow accent, I further suggest that you may be looking for a man with a high-pitched voice and stemming from elsewhere.'

'But,' said the Chief Inspector. He came to a halt for several seconds. 'But Angus Brown could be the liar.'

'If you think that, you may as well disbelieve the rest of his statement,' Henry said. I thought that he was taking care to exclude any trace of triumph from his voice.

Henry's argument might not be conclusive but at least he seemed to have clouded the issues very satisfactorily. The resulting silence allowed me to put my oar into the muddied waters. 'But why would Gus pick on me to incriminate?' I asked the general company.

'Good question.' Henry stopped and thought about it. The policemen waited expectantly.

'Because you were there,' Sergeant Ewell said suddenly into the silence. It seemed that I still had one friend in the enemy camp.

Henry shook his head. 'Because,' he said at last, 'whoever stabbed you is presumed to have come to steal the dog. But you already had the dog. You wouldn't have bribed Gus Brown to steal it from you and to stab you in the process. So, to his twisted way of thinking, your guilt would let him off the hook.'

Chief Inspector Ainslie was nodding in spite of himself. He caught himself at it and sat still. 'That's one way of looking at it,' he said. 'We assumed at first that there was an intruder and that he wanted the dog. But if that was so, we don't believe that the intruder was Angus Brown. It was the American whom he had met previously. Then, suddenly, we find him working for the other man, the associate. I find the picture of Mr Falconer introducing or mentioning Gus Brown to his associate unconvincing.'

'It's open to argument,' Henry said, 'that anybody looking for a disreputable rogue in this locality would sooner or later be referred to Gus Brown.'

'It's equally open to argument,' replied the Chief Inspector, 'that the intruder was the other associate, that he was after the money and that he took the dog as a ploy intended to mislead.'

'To mislead from what?' Henry asked. 'The dog was taken before the stabbing.'

'You may believe that,' the Chief Inspector said. 'I have to keep a more open mind. Let's suppose that the other associate, the man of finance, was after the money which had been taken by the shooting friend. He came here. He did not get his hands on the money and there was a fight in which Mr Cunningham was stabbed. Both parties would prefer that nobody asked awkward questions about the reason for his nocturnal visit, so one or the other faked the attempt to steal the dog.'

'Far-fetched and speculative,' Henry said.

'Perhaps,' the Chief Inspector said. 'But it's speculation which tidies up more of the anomalies than any other line of theorising. The simplest theory is often proved correct.'

I had been trying to get a word in but the two men had been ignoring me. 'Don't I get to say anything?' I asked.

'If you insist,' Henry said. 'But the Chief Inspector won't be interested in mere denials.'

I subsided.

'Take the alleged attempt to steal the spaniel,' said the Chief Inspector. 'What I've suggested furnishes one explanation which is at least credible. Can you suggest another?'

He was looking at me and I thought that he was watching me closely. I shook my head, trying not even to think about my idea of an implanted diamond. It had been a crazy thought in a mind fuddled by painkillers, but the Chief Inspector might find it more credible than I did. The harder I tried to exclude it, the more firmly fixed it became in my mind. I could only hope that none of the officers was telepathic.

'We've tried,' Henry said, 'but that aspect remains a mystery.'

The Chief Inspector made up his mind. 'And until that aspect of the mystery is resolved, we must go with the theory that most nearly explains it.'

'That we're all involved in one big conspiracy?'

The Chief Inspector shrugged. 'Not necessarily all of you,' he said. 'Dawn outings and a midnight confrontation. They could have happened outwith the knowledge of yourself and Mrs Kitts.'

140

So Beth and I were to be the chosen suspects. 'What happens now?' I asked.

'This is a working business,' Henry said. 'It took years to establish and there's a lot of money involved. You'd better be very sure of yourself before you take Mr Cunningham out of circulation. Or anybody else.'

'Then let's hope that it doesn't come to that,' the Chief Inspector said cheerfully. 'Note that I haven't said anything yet about taking Mr Cunningham into custody. We have been theorising. Now we need evidence. I have a search warrant with me. Much will depend on what we find.'

'You needn't even serve your warrant,' I said. 'Go ahead and search. You won't find any large sums of money.'

'Or luggage,' Henry said.

The Chief Inspector sat up and stared at him. 'What put luggage into your mind?'

'It's common knowledge,' Henry said, 'that Mr Falconer's luggage vanished from the hotel. If it had ever been found, the newspapers would have reported it.'

Ainslie relaxed. He was leaning forward as if about to struggle to his feet – no mean task from the low settee – when the door opened.

Beth came in. The hob ferret was riding comfortably on her shoulder. 'Sorry,' she said. 'I didn't know that you still had visitors. Shall I light the fire?'

'Don't bother,' I said.

'The post's come.' She dropped a few letters on the coffee table and turned to go.

'Hold on,' I said. It had all been happening too quickly. My thinking processes had seemed to be stunned. But her appearance kicked them back into life. 'I've told these gentlemen that they can search the place and welcome. I'll explain later. You might tell Isobel.'

Beth nodded hesitantly, realising that this was not the moment for a torrent of questions.

'And,' I said, 'you can leave His Nibs with me.'

'All right.' She detached the ferret from her shoulder and dropped him on to mine where he settled immediately. 'I just hope they don't make a mess, that's all.'

The door closed gently behind her. I looked at the Chief Inspector. 'Henry was wrong,' I said. 'Gus isn't as subtle as Henry suggested. He isn't subtle at all. In fact, he's the stupidest man I know. He uses bluster instead of brains. I've just realised why he's picked on me to drop in the shit. It's sheer spite. How would you like to get the truth out of him?'

'If we don't already have it,' Ainslie said slowly, 'then of course we want it.'

'I told you all that I remembered about his phone-call. I may have missed out a few words – unintentionally, Chief Inspector. You needn't look at me as though my flies were open. When insults are being traded one tends not to remember them verbatim. He called up to be abusive. He resented having to go on the run, as he thought, because of my interference. He got me damned annoyed. I was and am quite sure that Gus was my attacker, so for him to blame me for his troubles was a piece of damned impertinence. What's more, when he had to run off, he had the gall to dump his ferrets on me to keep for him. And after all that he was giving me dog's abuse. So the last thing that I said before I slammed down the phone was that I'd drowned his blasted ferrets in a bucket.'

'And had you?' the Chief Inspector enquired.

'No, of course not. This is one of them.' I put my hand up and tickled the ferret. He pushed his flat nose against my hand. 'I couldn't think of any other retort which would get through to him. I suggest that you get word to whoever's responsible for questioning

142

Gus Brown. Tell him to let slip that the ferrets are alive and well. Gus's dog and his ferrets are his only friends in the world. Get him thinking about what I might do if he goes on lying about me.'

Ainslie looked at me through half closed eyes. 'I've supervised the questioning of Mr Brown myself,' he said. 'I don't hold out much hope, but I'll try it – within reason. But I'm not going to convey what might be a message designed to turn him away from the truth.'

'How you handle him is your business,' I said. 'But you're welcome to suggest that I won't be pushing for the assault charge if he tells the truth now. Strike whatever bargains you like over that, I won't care just as long as we clear this up.'

He looked at me as though I had broken wind, but I had a feeling that it was for show. 'As you say, it's my business,' he said. 'We're going ahead with the search now. There will be more officers here within a few minutes. I want both of you to remain in this room. Sergeant Ewell will keep you company and make sure that nothing is . . . moved. Meantime, I'll be returning to Kirkcaldy and I might just have a word or two with Angus Brown. We'll get the truth out of him in the end,' he added grimly. 'But I can't promise that you'll like it.'

Another car with a team of officers must have been waiting nearby, because within a minute or two of his departure we heard a car in the drive, feet in the hall and female voices raised in protest.

Beth rejoined us a few minutes later. She was wheeling a trolley and I realised that lunchtime had already come and almost gone. The Sergeant looked tactfully away, trying hard to suggest that he was no more than a figment of our imaginations, but Beth had included him in the mugs of soup, crisp white bread with our home-made pheasant pâté and tea. He soon unbent and began to eat.

'Whatever else we have to put up with,' Beth said bravely, 'we don't have to starve ourselves.'

I found that my appetite had deserted me. 'What about Isobel?' I asked. I knew that others had to eat.

'There's a man going through her papers and she's far too busy standing over him to make sure that he doesn't put back any of her breeding records out of order. I'll take her something later. Now,' Beth said, 'what's going on?'

Henry glanced at me in warning. He gave Beth a Bowdlerised version of the Chief Inspector's words. Even so, she turned white.

Beth, perhaps in part because she looked impossibly young to be a sensible and married adult, sometimes gave me the impression of being a witless teenager, but she could keep her head in a crisis. She had a hard core of common sense and could sometimes make leaps of logic which outpaced me.

She made and daintily consumed a small sandwich before speaking. 'They usually suspect whoever finds a body, don't they?' she said.

'Usually,' Henry said.

'But in this case, surely it's the other way around? If Mr Falconer had been in the water for a week or two – there's no doubt about that, is there?'

We glanced at the Sergeant but he looked away.

'One would suppose that there was no doubt about that,' Henry said. 'You may be suspected of dropping the body into some convenient pond and then moving it to the Eden for more permanent disposal. The Chief Inspector was unspecific.'

'That's what I thought,' Beth said, 'although I don't see why we'd have waited around to find him again. But if we'd dropped him off the bridge a fortnight earlier, it would be an awful coincidence if he came drifting to our feet like that. Or does the Chief Inspector think that he was trying to accuse us from the grave?'

Sergeant Ewell continued to avoid her eye but he gave a faint shrug.

'Well then, the state of his clothes and . . . and the rest of him surely showed that he'd been going up and down with the tide for ages. Didn't it?'

We all looked at the Sergeant. He closed his mouth firmly at first and concentrated on spreading pâté on another slice of bread, but the habit of speech was too strong for him and he had become used to using us as his confidants. 'The pathologist thinks it's possible – no more than possible, mind – that somebody used an electric sander on the body.'

'I do have an electric sander,' I said, 'but they won't find any traces of skin or cloth on the disc.'

'From which,' Henry said gloomily, 'he will no doubt conclude that you have changed the disc.'

Beth put a hand to her face. 'There's a new disc in it,' she said. 'I was sanding down a cupboard door which I was going to paint. When I'd finished, the disc was worn out; so I put on a new one. Oh, John . . . !'

A tall man with a drooping moustache came in, carrying a small leather suitcase. He looked vaguely from me to Beth. 'Would this belong to either of you?' he asked.

'It's mine,' I said. 'I've had it for years.'

'There's a TWA sticker on it.'

'I've been to the States several times.'

'Ah? Well, it'll have to go to Forensic.' He wandered out again. Beth got up and closed the door after him.

'Let's look at this from the Chief Inspector's viewpoint,' Henry said, 'and see what we have to contend with.' He turned his sharp eyes towards Sergeant Ewell. 'You're not secretly taping this, are you?' (The Sergeant

145

looked blank and then shook his head.) 'Well, if you are and if anybody tries to edit what I'm going to say, we've three witnesses to the fact that I'm speaking hypothetically. We'll start from the assumption that the Chief Inspector believes you, John, to be the elusive shooting companion. Or, possibly, me.'

'You?' I said blankly. 'Do you mean it? You aren't just thinking of drawing the enemy's fire?'

'I'm not so stupid, nor so quixotic. Come to think, I would make a better suspect. I could spare the time and I haven't been ill for half the winter as you have. The Chief Inspector hasn't mentioned that possibility, but there are several other things which he hasn't seen fit to mention yet. If he's thinking along the lines which I would follow if I were in his shoes, he can't think that Isobel is wholly innocent. For all we know, he has another search warrant for my place.'

Henry looked again at the Sergeant, who looked away into the empty fireplace. 'Of course, we don't know what other lies Gus may have fabricated. Anyway, one of us – in the Chief Inspector's view – is Mr Falconer's shooting crony and knew or found out about the swindle. At the most propitious moment, he invites him back home for breakfast and a hot bath after a dawn wildfowling trip and drowns him in the bathwater. Thereafter he – or any permutation from the four of us – dresses him again, works him over with the sander and stows him somewhere wet, such as the small pond on The Moss, until he or they think that any traces of soap or whatever are beyond detection. Accept for the moment that, in order to support the eventual story, Anon was abandoned in or near St Andrews at about the same time. Then, much later, you, with some help from Beth, drop the body off the bridge before dawn on a rising tide, keep pace with it along the bank and wait for it to come ashore further upstream.'

146

'You make it sound sort of possible,' Beth said after an uncomfortable pause, 'but, if we'd done all that, why would we go to so much trouble to be helpful, identifying Anon and all that?'

Henry was speaking more slowly and I could see that he was struggling to stay ahead of his own argument. 'For the same reason that you made sure that the body was found. You wanted it confirmed that he was dead.'

'But why?'

'Damned if I know. You'd have to look inside the Chief Inspector's mind to answer that one,' Henry said helplessly. 'And know what stories Gus Brown's been feeding him.'

Sergeant Ewell's professional reticence broke down at last. He turned to face us. 'It isn't Bob's fault,' he said. 'Chief Inspector Ainslie, I mean. What you're up against, I think, is that one of my rivals for the next promotion vacancy works with him in Kirkcaldy. If he can make me look a Charlie for trusting you with the dog, his chances will be that much better. They think, between them, that the dog gie'd you the slip first time. You wanted it known that the man was dead so that you could get your hands on the dog. And I was fool enough to bring her back to you. That's what they think.'

It was difficult to know what to say. My mind went wandering. 'Is Chief Inspector Ainslie your brother-in-law?' I said. 'You referred to an inspector.'

The Sergeant sighed. 'I referred to what my wife said when he went up to inspector. What she said when he climbed another rung I wouldn't even repeat.'

Beth was sticking firmly to the mainstream of argument. 'It still doesn't quite make sense. Why does he think that we'd want another dog?' she demanded.

The Sergeant looked from one to another of us. 'You haven't guessed? It's because of the money. There's been

147

just no trace of it at all.' (I closed my eyes. I could guess what was coming.) 'They think that the money was used to buy a diamond or some other such thing, which was then implanted under the spaniel's skin, ready for the trip back to America.'

'But Isobel examined her,' Beth said. 'She was sure that there was no such thing.'

'Isobel's one of us,' Henry said tiredly. 'According to the Chief Inspector, she would have done the implanting.'

'Then I went and took her abroad,' I said. 'I can imagine how that looks to them.'

'And you came back with a whole lot of traveller's cheques,' the Sergeant said, 'signed with two whorls and a squiggle. Don't forget about that.'

'Only a thousand dollars,' I said.

'A thousand deposited in the local bank. That's all that they've traced so far. They're still looking.'

'It hangs together uncomfortably well,' Henry said. 'It explains everything except, perhaps, how we hoped to get the dog back into our hands. Whatever devious plot we had in mind must have been obviated by Sergeant Ewell's decision to bring her to us.'

'Henry,' I said, 'you're beginning to speak as if this was all true. You're forgetting that it's fiction.'

Henry looked at me reprovingly. 'You do me an injustice,' he said. 'If we can piece it together into a logical story, we'll be looking into the Chief Inspector's mind. And that should tell us what we need to find in order to disabuse that mind. I think . . . yes, I think that it's time you broke your promise and got in touch with Mr Rodgers's client.'

'I can't,' I said.

'You must. If you can account for your movements in the States, you can knock a large hole in that particular theory.'

'I've no way of contacting her.'

'Get in touch with Mr Rodgers. Ask him to get in touch with the widow and advise her of your predicament.'

I shook my head and let them think what they would. Even if Mr Rodgers could and would put me in touch with his client, I could only account for my movements by admitting that I had been present when Bubba was killed. And that I had run for it. And . . .

Beth was looking at me in consternation. I was past caring about anything else but I desperately wanted to ask whether she was envisaging me as a murderer or a philanderer.

Henry had not missed the signs. 'This isn't getting us anywhere,' he said quickly. 'Not that I'm convinced that anybody's going to get anywhere. Ainslie seems to have given up on looking for the financial wizard among the bankers – rightly, because that's not where he'd be found anyway.'

Sergeant Ewell had been regarding me with fresh suspicion but now he pricked up his ears and returned his attention to Henry. 'Why not?'

'Because any idiot can make money disappear in this day and age. A computer buff would only have to hack into the bank's computer. Thereafter, one method among many would be to change the name on the account. Suppose that an account in the name of John Smith at Two Eight Seven King Street suddenly became the account of John Smithson at Two Seven Eight Queen Street, who the hell's going to notice? The only physical record would be on the cheque books and bank cards, but even if he wasn't content to draw the money from the cash machine piecemeal he could transfer the account to a branch of another bank and withdraw it from there.'

The Sergeant was looking at Henry with the eyes of

a spaniel that sees a biscuit. Perhaps he could salvage his tarnished image through some smart, if second-hand, detective work. 'So who are we looking for then?' he asked.

'Somebody who knows Scottish Office procedures backwards. Grants Division of the Scottish Development Department or the Estates Department of one of the new towns. A spare-time computer fanatic, perhaps, or— '

The subdued warble of the telephone extension interrupted him. The Sergeant reached for it. 'I'd be expected to deal with any phone-calls,' he said apologetically. He read off the phone number into the mouthpiece and then listened intently.

'In case the call is from some confederate,' Henry said disgustedly, 'and we warn him to flee.'

But the call was evidently for the Sergeant. He listened for some minutes, returning occasional monosyllabic answers, and then hung up. 'That was my colleague in Kirkcaldy,' he said. His expression was that of a man who has eaten half a pie before finding a dead mouse in it.

'Your rival in the promotion stakes?' Beth asked.

'That's the man. Phoning me to crow. Mr Ainslie radioed ahead and told him to question Gus Brown. He took just the line he'd been told to take, or so he says, but Gus is sticking to his story.'

'It was a slim hope,' I said. The world seemed to be closing in around me. The cosy and self-contained life which I had wrapped around myself for the last few years was being pushed aside by savage reality which was itself unreal. 'Do you think he played fair?'

'There'd be nothing I could put my finger on,' the Sergeant said.

Henry leaned across to put a hand on my arm. 'Don't lose heart,' he said. 'Justice may suffer the occasional abortion, but she seldom miscarries. I doubt if they'll make a charge on present evidence and if they do I don't believe they've a hope of a conviction.' I flicked my eyes towards Beth. 'I know,' Henry said. 'A prosecution can be very hard on the innocent. Months in the pokey, financial hardship and permanent loss of reputation. But it won't come to that.'

The Sergeant was looking as worried as any of us. I hoped that he was concerned on my behalf and not only for his own promotion prospects. 'At least he was honest enough to pass on one small discrepancy,' he said. 'We'll see if you can make anything of it. My colleague told me that at one stage Gus Brown seemed to be on the point of changing his story. As you said, Mr Cunningham, the man's a fool. Whenever he was caught in a lie he resorted to bluster. He was rambling to the extent of being almost incoherent. Just once, he seemed to let slip that he hadn't really looked at the man who was with Mr Falconer by the Tay, the man who he'd been saying was yourself. He'd been too interested in the man's dog. My colleague moved on with his questions and then came back suddenly to the dog when he had Gus off-balance. Whatever else I think of him, he's clever at interrogations. "A snipey-nosed booger," Gus said, "and a damned queer colour." Then he shut his mouth again. But that didn't sound like a dog you'd be likely to have with you.'

Beth jerked upright in her chair. 'Lab or spaniel?' she asked.

The Sergeant scratched his head. 'Now there's a thing. According to Harry Jenkins – my colleague – Gus said something about the dog being "the colour of a copper's weskit". I took him to mean black, which would surely make it a Labrador. But we don't wear waistcoats. It's beyond me.'

I was almost afraid to ask the question. 'Could he have meant one of those orange waistcoats you put on when you're at the scene of an accident in the dark?' I asked.

'He could, I suppose,' said the Sergeant. 'But why would he? There never was a dog that colour.'

'Oh yes there was,' Beth said. 'Is that what you're thinking, John?'

That's exactly what I was thinking,' I said. The world was opening out again into a fair vista filled with sunshine and laughter, just beyond my reach. There was a doorway somewhere if I could only slip through it. 'We've seen just one dog which answered that description. And it belonged to a civil servant. He brought it to my masterclass, the Sunday after we found the body. And that same night I was attacked. What was his name? McConnach?'

'McConnelly,' Beth said. 'He asked me to call him Hugh.'

'Och,' the Sergeant said, 'we can't be going after a mannie just because he has a funny-coloured dog.'

'We can get more,' I said. I looked at Beth, who does most of my remembering for me. 'Who was that lady who used to judge at spaniel trials? She was something to do with Personnel at the Scottish Office. I think that she retired late last year.'

'Miss Cready,' said Beth. 'Elsie Cready. She lives in Bonnyrigg.'

'Any reason why I shouldn't phone her?' I asked the Sergeant.

'I'll look up the number for you,' he said. Later I realised that he was being cautious rather than helpful. We keep an Edinburgh directory as well as the one for Fife and Kinross. He found the number, pressed the buttons and then passed me the phone. The voice which came over the line was the voice which had once snapped at me that if my dog squeaked once more we would be put out of the trial.

I reminded Miss Cready of my existence and we had a short chat about old times. Retirement seemed to have mellowed her. When we had run out of gossip about the trials scene I said, 'I met a Mr Hugh McConnelly recently. You'd probably know him.'

'Now Mr Cunningham,' she said, 'you know that I can't give away any confidential information.' She spoke severely, but a year earlier she would have bitten my head off.

'I don't want you to tell me anything confidential,' I said. 'I'm trying to get in touch with him about a spaniel he rather fancied but which had been promised to somebody else. The other man can't take it now. I tried to phone Mr McConnelly last night but I didn't get an answer. I may have got the number wrong. I thought that if you could tell me which department he worked for I could ring him at work. You know, if anybody does, how many departments there are at the Scottish Office, scattered all through Edinburgh, and how difficult it is to get the switchboards to track somebody down.'

'Just phone the switchboard at St Andrews House,' she said. Before I had time to curse my luck, she went on, 'If there's more than one McConnelly – which I don't think there is – ask for the Computer Section.'

'Thank you very much,' I said warmly. On a sudden inspiration I added, 'Did I detect a trace of an American accent in his voice?'

'Possibly,' she said. 'You could have done, although I never noticed it.'

I thanked her again and rang off. 'Computer Section,' I said. 'And there's an American connection. He either did his degree or he's worked over there.'

'And who would be better placed to know the ropes and even to give one of them a pull now and again?' Henry said.

I caught the Sergeant's eye. 'So there's a much better suspect for you,' I said. 'If you find that he had a lady friend with a bum like an elephant's, you can thank us and then go and cover yourself with glory.'

He sat tight, looking troubled. 'It's no' just as simple as that,' he said. 'Not simple at all. Once they ha'e a good suspect, then yes, they can dig all around him, watch him, speak to his friends and neighbours, find where he was and when, who he knows and what's in his bank account. Usually, they'll come by the truth.'

'Well, then— ' Beth began.

'Wheesht a mintie and listen, lass. A job like that takes man-hours, hundreds and hundreds of them. And it canno' be done wi'out the suspect kens it, and if he's a man of substance he's kicking up hell and his friends are girning to the Chief Constable. It's not done lightly.'

'You're doing it lightly enough to me,' I said.

'That's as may be and it was never my choice; you know that surely. What I'm telling you is that there could be a dozen men of that description and wi' a queer-looking dog. The rest you've got is just supposition.'

'But he's the one who came to spy out where Anon was, just before we were visited in the night,' I said.

The Sergeant remained silent.

'Your superiors won't follow it up?' Henry said.

'They'll not get the chance. If I run to them wi' sic a tale, there's twa things can happen.' In his agitation, the Sergeant's careful speech was becoming broader. 'Either they laugh me out of the place and my promotion's gone forever. Or else they follow it up. They might do that but, if they did it, it'd be because somebody wanted me to fall in the stour. Just imagine the way I'd look if they did all that work and took all that stick only to find that the mannie was as innocent as a babe unborn. No,' the Sergeant finished firmly, 'I'll

154

need something more solid before I'll stake my chances of ever being an inspector.'

I felt sick. We had a theory which, in the light of our own knowledge, had to be more probable than the Chief Inspector's maunderings as inspired by Gus Brown; but to the police I still looked the better suspect. But my mind was still working. 'I remember one more thing,' I said. 'McConnelly was using an American pattern of dog-whistle. The one the dead man had around his neck was British made. That suggests that they liked each other's whistles and did a swap. Does that help?'

'Not a damn bit,' the Sergeant said. 'Now, if you could tell me why, if she didn't have an implant and if you were really stabbed in a fight over her, that damned wee springer bitch is so important . . . '

There was glum silence.

'They've only got to break Gus Brown,' Henry said suddenly. 'If he describes the man who hired him for the dognapping . . . '

'Likely it'll have been a voice on the phone,' said the Sergeant. He glanced at me. 'I told you what the landlady heard. That sounded awful much as if he was being hired over the phone.'

Henry began to argue but I had had enough. Let whatever was coming come. The mail was still on the table and, whatever the fates had in store for us, the business must continue to function for as long as it could. I picked up the top letter, looked for a moment at the American stamp, and then tore it open.

Hello there!
    All's well on this side of the pond. I'm getting hitched again next month. No flowers.
    Salmon of Glevedale – Anon to you – is doing great and sends her love. She asked me to send you a big lick and a photograph for your bedside. You

155

want one of the pups? If so, speak to Mr Rodgers.
Don't know what they are but they're cute as hell.

The letter was in an ornate script and was signed only
by a flourish. There was no address. It was postmarked
San Francisco.

In the accompanying photograph, Anon was to be
seen, proudly nursing a litter of six or seven puppies.
Even at that tender age – about two weeks, I judged –
the length of their noses was remarkable. Their brash
colour blazed out of the photograph.

I passed the letter and photograph to Henry, who
took one look and gave them to the Sergeant. Beth
got up and looked over the Sergeant's shoulder before
looking over to me and nodding. I saw the beginning
of one of her enormous grins. I was still too raw, deep
inside, to grin back yet; but I knew that a grin would
come.

'So that's why the bitch was important,' I said. 'At
a guess, he came out of the bathroom after drowning
his friend, to find that the bitch was being served by
the one dog in Christendom which could be described
unmistakably in about three words. Falconer was known
to have had a shooting friend. No matter how strongly
McConnelly denied being that friend or ever having
even met the man, sooner or later Anon was liable to
produce convincing evidence to the contrary.'

'A minute,' said the Sergeant. He picked up the
Edinburgh telephone directory and looked for the
number of St Andrews House.

I was still fitting the pieces together. 'He took her
along when he went to drop the body into the Eden,'
I said. 'He probably intended to drown her as well but
she got away from him.'

'Surely not!' Beth said. She tends to judge other
people by her own standards, and in her book not

even a calculating murderer could drown a pregnant spaniel.

The Sergeant's call lasted only a minute or so. 'Mr McConnelly left to go on leave, the day before Mr Falconer left the hotel,' he said. 'He never came back to his work. They had a postcard from Corfu to say that he was offering his resignation.'

Ten

There was no instantaneous lifting of suspicion. The police machine does not work that way. But while the search of the house ground slowly to a halt without discovering anything of more than passing interest to the searchers, the Sergeant spent the rest of the afternoon on our telephone, at our expense. He bypassed his rival colleague and his brother-in-law and spoke directly to a superintendent whose name I never knew. His manner was patient and apologetic, as though he hated to contradict a brother officer, but I could tell from the glint in his eye that he was enjoying himself.

By the evening of the following day all questions had been answered for the moment and statements signed. Suddenly we were at peace. Nobody had apologised, but as each officer made his final withdrawal there was a faint air, which pleased me just as well, of being glad to escape from an environment which had become oppressive.

Henry had left for another visit to Oban. Isobel had shared our meal and intended to stay late to remedy any disorder to her beloved breeding records, which gave Beth and me a rare chance to escape together for a visit to the hotel. Gus Brown, we heard, had been released with dire warnings about his future conduct. I had no great desire to be around when he came to collect his ferrets and yet I did not trust his spiteful nature. He could so easily come in the dark, with a box of matches . . . or a pair of ears from a myxied rabbit to drop in the rabbit pen. We did have a radio link to our 'alarm system', but an excitable dog barking at an owl could set the others off. I had too often come hurrying home to find nothing amiss.

We walked down the roadside verge together in the dark, arm in arm. The lights of the village were coming on as the shadow of the hills crept across the land. Not a breath stirred the trees.

'So that's it over,' Beth said happily.

'Until they make an arrest,' I said.

'When are you going to tell me about your trip to America? I know that something happened.'

I decided that I wanted to tell Beth all about it. Well, almost all. She would be suitably horrified by Bubba's death but she would understand why I had honoured my promise of silence. Jess's kind invitation would not be included in my report, but Beth's intuition was more than capable of assuming something of the sort. I preferred to account for every minute of my time. 'Soon,' I said. 'Whenever I can be absolutely sure that nobody else can overhear. Something rather dramatic did indeed happen.'

She squeezed my arm. 'You can tell me in bed tonight,' she said.

'I was beginning to have something else in mind for then. The calm after the storm brings out the best in me.'

'Mm. The best or the beast? You can tell me afterwards.'

The hotel, as usual, was fairly full. It had been a coaching inn on what was once a main road; it now maintained a standard which brought custom from many miles around. But half the faces were local and we attracted some curious glances. The search of our premises seemed to be common knowledge; the fact that we had been exonerated was less well known.

I had collected a gin and tonic and a pint of Guinness from the bar and we were heading for a quiet corner when I noticed a man, sitting alone at a table, who seemed to be avoiding my eye. There was something vaguely familiar about him but I was about to pass on when Beth said 'Hello!' in a pleased voice and the man looked up.

It was Sergeant Ewell, looking strangely unfamiliar in flannels and a well-worn golf jacket. Without the assurance of his neat uniform he was just another amiable nonentity, lost in the crowd and rather shy. Beth stopped beside him and he got to his feet.

'May we join you?' Beth asked him. 'There's only one vacant table and it's vacant because there's a howling draught there even when it's calm outside. We've sat there before.'

'Please do.' When we had sat down and Beth had rearranged the table to accept her bag, gloves and scarf, he said, 'You musn't think that I'm following you around. I just felt like a quiet pint.'

'I thought you lived in Cupar,' I said.

'I do. But I don't believe in drinking where I'm known. Other drinkers are either too friendly or not friendly at all. I've seen the outside of this place a dozen times in the last few weeks and my sister was coming over this way . . .'

'The Chief Inspector's wife?' Beth asked.

The Sergeant shook his head vigorously. 'That's my wife's brother, not my sister's husband. My wife was going to come along, but the sitter let us down.'

'A family celebration,' I suggested.

'Not quite. I daren't say anything to her yet, you understand,' he said earnestly, 'or she'll be counting her chickens and telling the neighbours. I just felt like a drink, myself, with the relief of it.' He glanced round and lowered his voice although nobody was paying any attention to us. 'It's all seeming conclusive at the moment. Mr McConnelly's house has been visited. He lived alone – near Kirkcaldy, would you believe? – and commuted to Edinburgh to work. Some bits of Mr Falconer's luggage were there and signs of a hurried departure plus a dog basket with bright orange hairs clinging to the blanket.'

'And a disc sander?' I asked. It seemed to me that the body would have been robbed of its fingerprints and other identifying marks before being committed to the water.

'That's gone for forensic examination. And I'll tell you something else. He had a lady friend with a . . . a generous backside, just the way you said. They've been seen together. We've still no idea who she is, though, or where she's got to now,' the Sergeant finished regretfully.

'It sounds enough to keep your bigwigs off our backs,' Beth said.

'More than enough. And there's more.' Sergeant Ewell looked from one to the other of us and then decided that we were tough enough to absorb some grisly tidings. 'They found what seemed to be a grave in the garden.'

'Not Mr McConnelly?' Beth said.

'No, not him,' the Sergeant said with a trace of a triumphant smile. 'His dog. Its skull had been smashed in. It had been there a couple of months but there was enough of it left to be sure that it answered your description. It even looked like the pups in yon photograph.'

'That's a shame,' Beth said. 'How could a man do that to his own dog?'

'There's some could do it to their own mothers,' the Sergeant said.

'So you're the golden boy, the toast of the Fife Constabulary?' I said.

161

'All but two of them,' he said, producing a reluctant smile. 'Aye, it may do the trick. You don't mind that I've stolen all of the credit?'

'Help yourself,' I said.

'And if you think of anything else . . . ?'

I laughed. He looked so modest but he had the nerve of the devil. 'You'll be the first to know,' I assured him.

'Aye. Well.' He looked past us and nodded. 'There's my sister waving at me. I'll need to go. Can I buy you a drink?'

'Wait until you get your promotion,' Beth said.

'And then I'll bring Champagne,' he said. 'I won't forget.' He finished his pint and got up. He hesitated as though he wanted to say something else, but after a moment he just wished us a good evening and slipped away through the throng.

Beth seemed to be looking in the direction in which he had disappeared. 'I'll be back in a moment,' she said. 'You sit here and finish your pint.'

I did as I was told, thinking that those were not the words which she would have used to excuse herself for the toilet. When I looked round, she had not after all buttonholed the Sergeant again but was in earnest conversation with Flora, the buxom lady who was presiding behind the bar.

Beth reappeared beside me several minutes later and dropped back into her chair. A worried look seemed out of place on her youthful features. 'I thought it was all over,' she said. 'But it can't be. You remember the girl who came to see you about buying a spaniel?'

'Dozens of them,' I said.

She shook her head impatiently. 'The special one with the big bum. Mr McConnelly's friend. I saw her at the bar a minute ago but she's vanished again.'

'Are you sure?'

'Positive. She's bleached her hair and done it differently, and she's not wearing those awful slacks, but there's no mistaking those hips. Flora says that she's been staying here for the past week. But she spends most of the time in her room and then goes out after dark. And – listen – she's got the end room, the one which gives a view towards Three Oaks. You can see the window from our upstairs and from the corner of the drive.'

'You think that she's watching us?'

'Flora says that she keeps a huge pair of binoculars on the window-sill. Should we phone the Sergeant?'

'If she's been watching us for a week, it can't be urgent,' I said. My guardian angel must have been in control of my tongue. 'Perhaps her boyfriend planted that story with Gus and she's watching on his behalf to see whether the blame's been shifted to us. Anyway, the Sergeant can't be home yet and he won't want to turn out again tonight, not if he only goes for a pint when he can get his sister to drive him. I'll ring him in the morning.'

Darkness had fallen when we left the hotel. We walked back, arm in arm again, quietly content with each other and with the sounds and scents of the night. I had taken the precaution of bringing a powerful torch. I had no wish to be jumped on in the dark by a resentful Gus Brown. But we reached home without incident.

Isobel was just preparing to leave. 'Did you see anybody you know?' she asked. Her question could have been taken to include the steatopygous lady but we were in no mood for endless speculation. We told her about the Sergeant and left it at that.

Beth and I were in no hurry for bed. Our mood was too good to curtail; and, thanks to my illness, the event had often failed to live up to our expectations. We made a last round of the kennels. Our residents seemed to be settled and in good health.

As we re-entered the house, Beth said, 'Now do I get to hear all about your American trip?'

'Yeah,' said a sudden voice. 'Me too.'

He had come out of the darkness behind us, a small man in a dark tracksuit.

His hair was now silver and receding and he had a neat moustache, silver-bright against a dark tan. His cheeks seemed broader. It took us a few seconds but, clued by some timbre in his voice, we got there together. 'Mr McConnelly!' Beth said.

We were in the light of the hall and he was standing in the open front doorway. In his hand was a weapon which had once been a shotgun – sixteen-bore, I judged, and sawn off with a crudity unworthy of a precision instrument. My stomach felt loose when I thought of the terrible damage that it could do at such close range. The other hall doors were closed and the latches had knobs rather than handles; no chance, then, of getting through in a single rush. Beth was clinging too tightly to my arm and if I shook her off it would signal my intention to attack.

I was impotent, the more so because impetuous action in Texas had almost thrown away my life and Jess's.

'All I want to know,' he said, 'is where the dog is now. The spaniel bitch. You know the one I mean.'

If McConnelly had already managed to leave the country, taking with him half or all the proceeds from the fraud, he had no reason to be searching for Anon. I thought then that whoever found Anon would also find Jess Holbright. The pattern of events, so tidy in my mind, turned itself inside out and I realised that we were in the most terrible danger. After surviving my folly in Texas it would be cruel to lose everything now.

164

The one remote avenue for escape would be to take his question at face value.

'When I took her to her new owner,' I said, 'the lady intended to disappear. But she sent me a photograph of the dog just the other day. The letter was postmarked San Francisco. That's all I can tell you.'

'San Francisco?' he said slowly. 'I'll be damned if that doesn't make sense. I never thought of him.' The drawl was strengthening as his mind raced ahead.

Beth began to speak. Her reasoning had followed the same path as mine, spurred by the accent. She had reached the truth a few seconds too late to see its implications. I squeezed her arm, trying to stop her, but it was too late. 'It's your wife you're trying to find,' she blurted out. 'You're not Mr McConnelly. You're Mr Falconer.'

There was a momentary silence so heavy that I thought I heard the floorboards creak.

'Yeah,' he said at last. The Texan accent was back at full strength. 'She thought I was dead. I couldn't risk a letter or a call. And I lost too much time, using Hugh's ticket to Corfu and covering my tracks and coming back to make a play for the dog and all like that. By the time I'd made it home she was gone and I couldn't stick around asking questions.' He sighed. 'I'm sorry,' he said, with what seemed to be genuine regret. I turned slowly, as if to put myself between him and Beth. But I was also putting her between me and the stairs. If I pushed her hard I would at the same time be pushing myself towards the gun. With a little luck, she might be up the stairs before my corpse was out of his way. Given fantastic luck, he might not yet have put off the safety catch.

Beth had got there at last. 'You don't have to . . . to do anything drastic,' she said quickly, in a very high voice. 'Lock us in the shop. It's secure. You can get away.'

'I could,' he said. 'But so long as they all think I'm dead, they'll go on looking for the wrong guy. And that's the way I want it. Too bad for you!'

He lifted the gun. Beth had put her arms round me. She was almost squeezing the breath out of me and there was nothing that I could do but take her in my arms. It was all that I wanted to do. If I had to die, it was the way that I wanted to go.

There came an awful noise. It was not as loud as a shot. It was hardly as loud as a sigh. It was followed by louder, stranger noises.

I looked round.

Instead of the man, the girl with the big hips was standing in the doorway. I knew her immediately, despite the blonde hair and the loose leather coat which half hid her figure. She had possessed herself of the sawn-off gun but seemed uncertain how to handle it, which made it almost as frightening as when it had been in the man's hands.

The man was down on his face at her feet. The handle of a knife protruded from his back. I knew enough anatomy to judge that if it had not found his heart it was very close to it. Even so, he twitched and made small noises for a few seconds before the absolute stillness of death took over. It reminded me, sickeningly, of Bubba.

Beth had looked once and looked away. I could feel her getting the shivers. We could do without an attack of hysteria now. I could not bring myself to slap her but I took her by the elbows and gave her a small shake. She stilled and began to pull herself together, but she faced my chest, refusing to look at the woman or the dead man.

The woman seemed to be in a daze, but neither of guilt nor of compunction. She was smiling, and this time she took no trouble to hide her crooked teeth.

Her eyes were far away. She had some of the look of a woman after sex but there was something else, too many other things. Except for the smile, which was half a snarl, she might have said a passionate farewell to a lover. Or come to the end of a long road. Now, I thought, she was starting again from scratch and totally unsure how to begin.

Her eyes found their focus. 'Mr Cunningham,' she said. 'Do forgive my coming without an appointment.' I thought for a moment that she was resorting to macabre humour. Then I realised that she was disoriented and that her uncertain mind was throwing back to her up-bringing.

'You're very welcome,' I said, shakily but with sincerity.

Her smile became friendlier, but the snarl snapped back into place as soon as I moved. The gun jerked up. 'Keep still,' she said. We froze, all three of us.

Beth, still looking away, had found a voice of sorts. And she said the damnedest thing. She said, 'Would you like a cup of tea?'

It turned out to be the right question. The woman stirred. The gun was still pointing in our general direction but she seemed to be only half aware of it. 'I'd just love a cup of tea,' she said.

With a dangerous wave of the truncated muzzles she gestured us into the kitchen.

Seconds later, I found myself sitting in one of the deep fireside chairs. The woman half sat on the table, watching Beth as she busied herself with the kettle and teapot. I guessed that Isobel must have made herself a hot drink, because the kettle came to the boil immediately.

'Please,' I said. I spoke slowly and clearly as if to a child. 'Do you mind not waving that gun around? Better take your finger outside the trigger-guard. We're not going to jump you. We're grateful. You've just saved our lives.'

She looked down vaguely at the gun but she did as I had said, pointing it at the floor. 'I won't shoot you unless you make me,' she said. 'And I'm quite used to guns. Hugh . . . ' Her voice, which had been husky, broke for a moment. 'I think that this was one of his. That animal out there kept it.'

I let out a breath of relief and I heard Beth do the same.

Beth poured tea. The woman stood back while Beth put a cup on the table and handed me a mug. She went back to the worktop for biscuits.

The woman looked at her watch. 'That's good,' she said more calmly. 'Thank you so much. They'll have stopped supper at the hotel and I've a long way to go.'

Beth took her own cup and sat down opposite to me. 'There's something I don't understand,' she said gently. 'I think I can work out the rest of it, but why were you watching this house? Did you know that he was going to come here?'

'I thought that he might. I was guessing.' The woman looked at her watch again. Instead of moving smoothly her eyes flicked. Her mouth still had a twitch and her face showed traces of both tears and sweat. To have killed the murderer of her lover was a profound enough emotional experience for any woman. It had brought her to some brink. I hoped that Beth would say nothing to push her over the edge.

'Well, why not?' she said at last. 'I've time in hand and they'll piece it together anyway. I was going to marry Hugh McConnelly but that . . . that garbage out in your hall killed him.' The look which crossed her face made me shiver.

'For his share of the money?' I asked.

'No. Hugh did the money thing and he made sure of

his share. I've been holding it ever since. But, you see, Hugh knew his real identity and Dave couldn't take that.' She paused in thought for a moment but when she went on again she was still rambling. 'I'll just go on calling him Dave, that's how Hugh referred to him. I still don't know his real name for sure, though I think it may have been Holbright. Hugh said that Dave was compulsively secretive. He didn't trust anybody. I knew a little about him from Hugh. He didn't know about me, which was lucky for me. But all that secrecy didn't do him any good in the end, did it?'

'Not a damn bit,' I said.

'Right,' she said. The terse agreement sounded off-beat in her prissy voice. 'Just sit there, please, and don't move.' She lifted her broad hips off the table and walked into the hall. I heard a grunt. She came back looking less thunderous. I was sure that she had kicked the dead man.

'He's bled on to your nice carpet,' she said. 'That's a shame. When Hugh stopped turning up for our dates, I knew at once that he was dead and who'd killed him. I was sure of it before you'd even found the body. I went out to Hugh's cottage but there was no sign of either of them.'

'Nor of Hugh's dog?' I asked.

She shook her head impatiently. 'Hugh had put his dog into kennels, ready for his trip abroad. And what the newspapers said about the body didn't fool me for a moment. They were much the same build, the two of them – Hugh often lent him clothes.

'I couldn't go to the police without admitting that I'd been an accessory. And I had no way of tracing the bastard – forgive the language,' she added daintily, 'but that's what he was. Then I read in the paper that you'd been stabbed when there was an attempt to steal the spaniel. Dave had to be behind it, but I still can't think why he wanted the dog so much. He was fond of the spaniel, so Hugh said, but that didn't explain it. Dave wasn't the sentimental sort.'

'The spaniel bitch was carrying the pups of your boyfriend's very distinctive dog,' I said.

She nodded, understanding. 'That would do it,' she said. 'Dave was obsessive about making a clean break, Hugh said. But Hugh never thought that Dave would kill him. And, afterwards, I suppose Dave couldn't risk any evidence linking the two of them. That could have turned fraud into murder, if he was ever caught. Couldn't it? And fraud can be much more difficult to prove.'

'He certainly took that danger very seriously,' I said. 'He even took the risk of bringing Hugh's dog here to my masterclass.'

'It wasn't so much of a risk,' she said. 'No more risky than being somewhere else. If you change your hair and your habits and the way you dress, go somewhere you're not known and call yourself Mr Smith or Miss Jones, nobody cares a damn who you are. I've proved that. If he'd met anybody here who knew him or Hugh, he could have turned around and gone away.'

'But why did he add to the risk by using Mr McConnelly's name?' Beth asked.

'Because it's well known that I insist on inoculation certificates,' I said. Now that we knew most of the story, the remainder was almost explaining itself. 'He wanted a dog that knew him and would work for him. McConnelly had left his dog in kennels ready for his holiday. He collected the certificate from the boarding kennels along with the dog and it had Hugh McConnelly's name on it. Although what good he expected to get out of the visit . . . '

Beth looked stricken. 'When you sent us off to practise, he seemed curious about the spaniel. So I showed her to him. Does that make it my fault that you were stabbed?'

'No way,' I said. 'You just made it a bit easier for him to brief Gus Brown where to find her.'

Our visitor had been following us. Her brow was creased in thought. 'So what became of Tang?' she asked.

'Tang?'

'Hugh's dog. He called him Tangerine.'

'I can see why he would,' I said. 'I'm afraid Tang's dead. We heard an hour ago that his body had been found, buried in Mr McConnelly's garden. I'm afraid that he – Dave – kept Tang just long enough to use him as an excuse to study the layout here. Then he killed him. He seems to have been as ruthless with dogs as he was with people. When I took the bitch to the States, he had somebody waiting. Damned nearly got his own wife killed.'

'From what Hugh said, that mightn't have worried Dave a lot. He cared about his wife but he cared a damned sight more about his own skin. He was the lowest sort of rat.' She paused, sipped tea with her little finger crooked and looked thoughtfully at the door. I decided that she was wondering whether to go out and kick the corpse again. Apparently she decided not to bother. 'Anyway, Hugh had a friend living in Fife.'

'The thickset man who brought the gun to the Stoneleigh Hotel?' Beth asked.

The muzzles of the gun stilled, pointed somewhere close to Beth's feet. 'You're not thinking of making trouble for him? He didn't know anything.'

Beth shook her head dumbly.

'Forget him. All he did was to deliver the gun, and to help me a little, afterwards. He knows nothing. He'd been in the States. He and Hugh first met when Hugh was studying in Dallas. He put me in touch with a private detective in San Diego, a man who he said could be trusted. He cost a bomb, but I had Hugh's money, remember.

'Hugh had never told me where Dave came from. But Dave told Hugh and Hugh told me the story of Langtry, Texas, and how Judge Roy Bean fell in love with a picture of the Jersey Lily and wrote to her all the time, but she never visited Texas until the year after the judge died. Only Hugh said that the place was named Langtry before Judge Bean ever arrived there.' She paused and gave a little sigh for another legend destroyed. 'Starting from there, he looked around to find where Dave's wife had been living. He heard about a shooting. The woman was exonerated, but she'd moved away immediately afterwards. And he – my detective – found out some other things. The spaniel – Salmon – had arrived there just before the man was shot, while you were away from here.'

'You were watching us?'

'Yes, of course,' she said, looking surprised. 'Whenever I could. He'd vanished and I wanted to find him more than I've wanted anything on this earth. I thought that he'd gone abroad and it seems that I was right but that he came back. You were my last link with him in this country. There was something in the papers about you taking the dog out to the States and I thought that my last link had broken. Then one more thing my detective found out was that somebody else in the same line of business had been hired to find out where the wife had gone. But she'd covered her tracks very cleverly.

'Thinking about it, I guessed that his wife was afraid that somebody would come after her so she'd run off with the money. The thoughtless swine hadn't even bothered to tell her that he was still alive, not even while he was contacting some roughneck to lie in wait

172

for the spaniel. When he turned up at last, she was gone and his dog with her.

'For all I knew, he might have decided not to bother. He had other money now and there are plenty of women who'll take up with a man who can spend. But he might care for his wife enough to look for her, and if anybody knew where she'd gone it might be you. If I could work that out, he could. And then again, I had to be somewhere.' she sighed again. 'One place was as good as another now that Hugh was dead. There didn't seem to be much else to do with my life. I might just as well be here as anywhere, watching in case he came to find out where his wife had gone. Now that he's dead, I'm free.'

'What are you going to do now?' Beth asked.

Beth's question, I could tell from the fear in her voice, was directed towards the question of what she intended to do with us, but our guest considered it carefully. 'God knows,' she said at last. 'It's a clean slate. I've money but I've no ties, no job and no man any more. I might go and be a missionary or something. Perhaps it's time I did some good in the world – other than ridding it of . . . him.'

We fell silent. I was thinking about the slim chance which had brought her to our door at the right moment and how near I had come to repeating the impetuous mistake which had nearly proved disastrous in Texas.

She looked at her watch again and then at me. The gun came up and for a gut-watering moment I expected a load of shot. 'Time's running out,' she said. 'Would you please empty your pockets on to the floor.' I looked at her blankly. 'Keys,' she said in explanation.

I gave her my keys and restored my few other oddments to my pockets.

'We don't even know your name,' Beth said.

'That's true. Now, where's this shop?'

The shop, so called, was an attached stone outbuilding which had come into its use because visitors sometimes bought a spaniel on impulse without having a bed or a lead or even a scrap of dogfood for it. It had become a recognised supplier of training aids for the district. I led the way out of the kitchen by the outside door and across a small porch and we stood back while she fiddled with the good security lock. The stock was no more valuable than the contents of the house, but my guns lived in the workshop and junk room behind the shop.

I led Beth in, switching on the light. The woman followed us in and took a look at the barred window. Then the door slammed on us. 'The keys will be on the table,' called her voice.

Beth thanked her. The politeness of our exchanges seemed to be infectious.

We could hear her moving around, faintly, somewhere in the house. 'What's she doing?' Beth asked me in a whisper.

'I think she's searching the body. He probably has his share of the money on him, or a clue to where it's waiting.'

Beth shivered.

We heard her voice once more. In a way, it was the most remarkable courtesy of all. She came back to the door. 'Do you mind if I use your bathroom before I go?' she asked.

We looked at each other in surprise. 'Not at all,' I said.

We heard water running and the toilet flushed. Then all was silence.

'Mad,' Beth said in a small voice. 'Quite mad. I can understand her doing what she did. I . . . I hope I'd have the strength to do the same if somebody killed you. But to be so polite about it, that's unnatural.'

'I think she's walking a sort of tightrope,' I said. 'She

174

needs something familiar to hang on to. When she isn't under stress, she's polite and considerate.'

'Well, I still say it's not natural. Can you get us out of here? Shoot the lock off or something?'

I pointed out that my guns were in a steel safe and the keys were on the kitchen table.

'We're here for the night then?'

'I'm afraid so,' I said. 'But we don't have to be uncomfortable.' A stock of dog-nests had been delivered only a few days before. I made a comfortable pile of them in a corner, out of the way of any draughts, and switched off the light. We sat down and then lay back, pleasantly intimate.

'Now,' said Beth's voice, 'you can tell me all about what happened in Texas.'

Perhaps it was the relief at evading death, but my body was sending me messages. 'I can think of something much more interesting to do,' I said.

Beth turned in the circle of my arms and kissed my nose. 'Tell me first,' she said comfortably.

She listened intently as I spoke into the darkness. Her sympathies were entirely with Jess. Beth herself would not have hesitated to kill a man who was going to shoot Jason. And while we spoke, our passion crept out of hiding.

We were keyed up. Even after we had made love, gently and successfully, sleep was slow to come. The dog-nests had not been designed for human use and our minds were too alert after the events of the day. I was exhausted but whenever I fell into a doze Beth's fidgets jerked me awake again.

'Empty your head,' I told her at last. 'Imagine that you're hunting for fleas on a black velvet curtain.'

We settled down again. I was falling at last into a deep sleep when she sat up suddenly. 'I got one of them,' she said sleepily. 'Take it from me.'

175

★ ★ ★

We heard the scream when Isobel arrived in the morning, but before we could attract her attention she had dashed off down to the village to phone the Sergeant about the body in our hall. As she explained later, her detective plays had taught her that nothing must be touched; but I believe that she had been afraid to penetrate deeper into the house in case she found Beth and me, equally dead and similarly gory. We had to wait another half-hour before we were released. By then, it was eventually learned, the lady's plane had already left Gatwick.

She sent us a Christmas card from Beirut.

We saw her once more, in a TV news item about the famine in Ethiopia. She was among a group of relief workers and seemed to be enjoying herself, striding around and bossing the natives. Her hair was cropped short but there was no doubt that it was the same woman. Against her dark tan the crooked teeth flashed white as she smiled and smiled.